Seasons of Love

(Part Two)

Autumn's Story

Written By: Quisha Dynae

Chapter 1

Sweat was pouring down Autumn's face, and her shirt was drenched in sweat as she let the beat of the multiple bass drums flow through her body. Her back was straight as her arms extended to make a figure eight above her head, and then she twirled her flag behind her back, going over the routine in her head.

One and two and three and four and... She repeated over and over again until the last note from the trumpets, tubas, and saxophones were played.

It was mid-August, and Autumn was currently in band camp for the Johnson C. Smith Golden Bulls. She relaxed when given the command "at ease" by Sammy the drum major and then headed to get herself some water.

She hated the stares she received from other members of the auxiliary squad and even the dance team. All of them hated her for the simple fact that she was with the star of the track team, Mason. She had heard the rumors of him messing around with others, but she had no proof. She was about tired of his ass anyway. Anytime he didn't get his way, he had a habit of putting his hands on her. No one knew because she was too embarrassed to tell anyone. She knew that her sisters, and even her grandmother, would tear Johnson C. Smith up looking for Mason. She was the baby in the family, and they didn't play about her. Her sister, Summer, was currently pregnant, and she knew that even she would be on a warpath.

Her and Mason met during her sophomore year, and she was now a junior majoring in English and Language Arts; her dreams were to be an eighth grade English teacher.

"Hey, Autumn girl, where is Mason; he didn't come watch you today?" Katrina, the captain of the dance team, asked.

Autumn rolled her eyes as she responded, "You the one always on his dick, so you should know."

"Girl, bye, he must be with another bitch." Jalisa laughed, chiming in.

"Whatever." Autumn walked away from the foolishness. She didn't have time for the bullshit. Those bitches were always trying to ruffle her feathers to get a reaction out of her. There was a zero tolerance for fighting during practice, as well as on and off the field period. She couldn't afford to be kicked off the squad because she got a full band scholarship. Without it, she wouldn't be able to pay for school. Not to mention, her sisters, Summer and Wynter, plus her grandma, Maggie, would be so disappointed in her. Her sisters made something of themselves, and she refused to be the disappointment of the family.

Five o'clock had come before Autumn knew it, and she was headed to her dorm room.

"Autumn, hold up," Hannah, Autumn's roommate, called out to her. She was a clarinetist in the band and Autumn's best friend.

"Hey, girl." Autumn slowed down so that Hannah could catch up.

"I heard what them hoes said. Don't worry about them, girl. They are just jealous," said Hannah, giving Autumn a subtle smile.

That was true. Bitches were jealous of Autumn. She was sexy and smart. Autumn was five feet six inches tall with legs for days. She had smooth, caramel skin, full, pink lips, chinky eyes, and long, thick, natural hair and eyebrows. Her body was well developed with C-cup breasts, a small waist, and a big, round ass that niggas dreamed about.

"I know they are, girl. They just aggy as fuck," said Autumn as they walked into Greenfield Hall where they were housed.

That was what attracted Mason to Autumn. She was a rare breed, and she was loyal. Their relationship wasn't bad at first. Mason was a gentleman when they first met. He took her on dates, they ate together in the student union, and they sat for hours together in the library studying; in other words, they were glued at the hip. She first noticed a change in him during spring track season. It was like track was the only thing that mattered to him.

He couldn't balance her and the team. Mason was a track star and was number one in his division. He ran multiple events: the 400 meters, 200 meters, and the 4x200 meters relay. He was conceited and rightfully so. She just needed him to learn how to divide his time. She understood track was important to him, and she was happy that he had so much success in doing what he loved, but she needed time too. She didn't know how much she could take before she left him.

"I'm going to take a shower first. I need to be headed to the library to study," Hannah told Autumn as she began to gather her things for a shower.

"Oh that's cool. Go ahead; I will call my sister back while you're in there," said Autumn while holding her phone realizing that she missed a call from Summer.

Autumn stripped out of her sweaty clothes, and then sat on her bed to make that call.

"Hello."

"Hey, sis, what you and my nephew doing?" Autumn asked once Summer answered the phone.

"Girl, you know he be kicking my ass sometimes. Between him and Robert's ass, I don't know who is worse," Summer answered, speaking of her unborn child and boyfriend.

Autumn had two sisters: Summer and Wynter. All three of them grew up close, and they're even closer to this day. Since their parents died, it had just been the three of them plus their grandma, who they called Memaw. Being the youngest of the three, Autumn looked up to her sisters and didn't know where she would be right now if it wasn't for them. They were the ones who stayed up day and night helping prepare her for the SAT. They went to most of her marching band practices and all of her games giving her pointers on how to become better.

Autumn and Summer talked until Hannah walked out of the bathroom. Autumn let Summer know that she would be by soon. After hanging up, Autumn went to take her shower.

After Autumn was finished with her shower, she stepped out and was surprised to see Mason sitting on her bed with a big ass grin on his face. She rolled her eyes at him not wanting to deal with him right now.

Chapter 2

Mason Dixon, the track star, came from a two-parent home. His parents, Rhonda and Terry weren't rich, but they had enough to be comfortable. Since he was five years old, he ran track for the Charlotte Runners, a team that his father started and coached alongside his mother.

Both of his parents were always hard on him. His father was a retired colonel in the United States Air Force. His mother ran track at Shaw University but became a stay at home mother to their only son when she graduated. When Terry would be away, Rhonda would coach the team. Needless to say, she trained a star.

He was punished at a young age for not placing in the top three. As he got older, around high school, they expected no less than first place. Rhonda and Terry trained him to be the best, and that's what he became.

Mason loved running, but as he got older and his parents expected more, he found other ways to strengthen himself when practicing wasn't working on men that were better than him. Don't get it wrong, Mason was a beast, but some of these men from other states were awesome. He would breeze through regular season and states, but regional was a struggle at times, which was why he sometimes needed a little push.

"Girl, get your ass up. I already missed my girl's practice because of you," said Mason, speaking to his side chick that he smashed every once in awhile.

Rachel smacked her lips not giving a damn about what he was saying.

"I don't even see why you are still with her as much as you fuck me," she said while swinging her legs over on the side of the bed so that she could stand up. She walked to the bathroom to freshen up.

"What I tell you about that shit, Rachel?" He smacked her hard on the ass, making her yelp before he said, "You know what it is, so don't complain." He grabbed his pants and began getting dressed since he had already taken a shower.

Mason really did love Autumn. She was a dime in his eyes. Autumn was everything, but he was also a young man who hadn't grown yet. He thought fucking around made him "the man". As long as Autumn didn't know, things were cool. Yeah, he knew people talked. Autumn was always in his ear about shit that circulated around campus, but he shut that shit down with a shot of good dick, and Autumn fell for it every time.

Once Rachel was gone, he made his way to Autumn's dorm.

Mason wasn't only the star of the track team, he was also a heartbreaker. He was a pretty boy. His smooth light skin and curly hair attracted the women. The fact that he ran track and worked out often had his body built like a god. His perfect smile had the woman wetting their panties whenever he walked by.

"Heeeyyyy, Masooon," a group of girls sang and then giggled as he passed by.

Mason smiled in return at them and then responded, "What's up ladies?" but kept walking to get to his girl.

Walking into her dorm, he got a lot of stares from the women standing around. The first person he noticed was Katrina. He let out a sigh as she approached him. He wasn't in the mood for her shit. She was one person that he hated he smashed. She had him once, and apparently that wasn't enough. Her ass was thirsty, and he thought it was sad.

"Hey, Mason. What's up with you?" She stepped in front of him when he tried to walk past her.

She placed her finger on his chest, and he smacked it away. She heard snickering behind her and turned around to give her friends "the eye". You know, the one when you told someone to shut the fuck up with your eyes.

"What the fuck do you want, Katrina?"

"I want you, baby. You haven't got up with me since last year." She pouted.

"Well, what does that tell you?" he asked with a raised brow.

"You still stuck on that bitch with the nappy ass hair? I should get her ass kicked off the squad."

Mason grabbed her arm hard as fuck and pulled her to the corner. "Bitch, stop disrespecting her. She hasn't done shit to your ass. And I promise if she gets kicked off the team, I will whip your thirsty ass myself." He let her go as she stared at him with wide eyes.

"Fuck you, Mason."

She stormed off as he yelled, "You wish hoe!" before continuing to Autumn's room.

He knocked on the door and waited for an answer. A few seconds later, Autumn's roommate, Hannah, answered the door.

"Hey, Mason, I was just leaving, but she is in the shower. Come in and wait," Hannah said as she headed out.

"'Preciate it," he responded before walking into the room, closing the door, and getting comfortable on Autumn's bed.

Five minutes later, Autumn stepped out of the bathroom and rolled her eyes upon seeing Mason sitting on her bed smiling. When he saw that she had an attitude, his smile dropped before saying, "Damn, who shitted in your coffee?"

Autumn grabbed her lotion and sat on the bed to apply it to her body.

"You apparently. Why Katrina keep messing with me? You fuck her or something?" Autumn looked up into his eyes.

"Hell naw, man. Ain't nobody fuck that bitch!" he exclaimed.

Autumn gave him the side-eye as she continued to apply lotion to her body and said, "Whatever; every time we in practice that bitch has something to say to me. You must have gave her hope or something."

"Nah, baby, she probably just wishes she could have what you have." He removed her towel and eyed her lustfully.

He licked his lips as his dick swelled just watching her hands caress her own body. He moved her hair out the way and turned her head with his finger so that he could kiss her lips.

"All I want is you, and you know that," he whispered in her ear as his hand opened her legs wider so that he could have access to play with her pussy. She let out a soft moan as soon as he applied pressure to her clit.

"You always do this, Mason. Sex will not make me forget about these hoes that approach me," she moaned out as her head fell back when his finger glided into her honey pot.

"Nah, you just sexy as fuck. I can't help myself," he said as he grabbed her breast and squeezed it softly with his free hand.

She swung her leg over his and rotated her hips as she felt her orgasm surfacing.

"Let that shit go, babe."

As soon as he said the words, her legs trembled, and she let loose. Mason then stood up and removed his clothes as she laid back and waited on him. She licked her lips as his smooth, light brown dick sprang up once he was naked.

Autumn thought Mason was the sexiest nigga thus far that she'd talked to. He was smart and talented too; that's why she stayed with him despite his flaws.

Mason climbed between her legs giving her a peck on the lips before placing her legs over his shoulders and entering her slowly. He was doing what he always did, fucking her into forgetting.

Chapter 3

Autumn woke up from the nap she took after getting her back blown out. She looked over and smiled as she saw Mason and his sexiness under the cover. She looked at the time and realized that he needed to get up and get dressed before her roommate came back. She didn't think her friend would lust over her man, but to be sure, she always made sure that he was dressed when she came in.

"Babe, get up."

She nudged him with her elbow, causing his eyes to lazily open before saying, "What time is it?"

"It's time for you to get up before Hannah comes back." She got out the bed and waited for him so they could go into the bathroom together. Once he was up, they took a quick shower before getting dressed.

"What you up to tonight?" Autumn asked as he was putting his shoes on.

"I'll probably hit up the gym. After that, I'm not sure. Probably just chill with my boys or something; nothing major." He finished and then stood, pulling her up with him and circling his arms around her waist.

She placed her arms around his neck before pecking him on the lips, before saying, "You love me?"

"You know I love your sexy ass," he responded before kissing her lips again and then her forehead before letting go and heading for the door.

Autumn plopped down on her bed letting out a long breath of air. Hannah walked through the door and saw the worried look on her friend's face and said, "Girl, what he do?"

"The usual. He swear he hasn't messed with ol' girl, but I just don't believe it," said Autumn as she sat up on the bed.

"You know everything he does, if anything, will come out eventually," Hannah told her as she placed her books on her desk.

"You are so right," Autumn replied.

"Look, let's go out tonight; we can go to Stache House, the hookah lounge. I heard it has a nice crowd on Thursday nights," Hannah said as she bounced onto Autumn's bed.

"I don't know, Hannah."

"Why not? Girl, come on; stop sitting in this room thinking about his ass."

Autumn thought about it for a minute and agreed to go. She really did need to get out. She was scared to go out sometimes; she knew how jealous Mason could get and didn't want to see that side of him again.

Autumn looked over at the clock and realized it was already eight o'clock. They both decided to go ahead and get ready so that they could head out.

Two and a half hours later, they pulled up to Stache House off South Boulevard and parked the car. Autumn stepped out the car and checked her reflection out in the window. She looked amazing in a pair of mustard skinny jeans with a black crop top shirt that read 'Queen' across the front in gold letters. She looked down at her mustard and black striped colored pumps and was satisfied with her outfit. She had her thick, curly tresses up in a gigantic poof ball so that you could see her facial features. She had a pair of big gold Ankh earrings in her ear.

Once satisfied, they headed toward the back of the line. It was about fifteen people in front of them. Autumn heard someone call her name. She looked around before her eyes landed on Ka'ron. Ka'ron was a friend of the family who was good friends with her sister, Summer, and her boyfriend, Robert. She smiled big as she walked back to the front where he and one of his homeboys were standing.

"What's up, baby girl?" Ka'ron pulled her into a hug, causing her to hug him back.

Autumn had a crush on Ka'ron since they were younger, and she hated when he called her baby girl or lil' mama. It made her feel so young, and she wanted him to look at her as more than some young girl. She knew that if he wanted her, she would most likely leave Mason. He was starting to trip anyway, so it would be no love lost.

When she pulled away, she introduced Hannah to Ka'ron and his friend whose name was Greg.

"Y'all don't have to wait in line; come in with us." Ka'ron placed his hand on Autumn's lower back and led her into the lounge with Hannah following close behind. She walked right beside Ka'ron until he walked into his VIP section and sat down. He gently pulled her down beside him and asked, "You drinking?"

"We were really just coming for the hookah, but since you asked, let me get Cîroc and cranberry." As she finished her sentence, Ka'ron was waving down a waitress.

"Hey, Ka'ron, what can I get you?" she asked as she eyed Autumn with an attitude. Autumn sat unbothered with her long legs crossed. Ka'ron unintentionally placed his hand on Autumn's thigh as he ordered two bottles of Cîroc with cranberry and orange juice. He also ordered two Budweisers for him and Greg.

"Damn, you used to mess with her or something?" Autumn asked.

"Nah, she just want ya boy." He stared into her eyes before licking his lips and saying, "You look good as fuck, Autumn. I hope that boyfriend of yours is treating you right 'cause you are of age now." He looked her over once again, causing her to blush and look away.

The waitress came back and placed their bottles on the table along with four glasses and a bucket of ice. Ka'ron then ordered the hookah, which he originally forgot about, and that was brought to them quickly. Autumn looked over to check on her friend and saw that she was having a good time talking to Greg. She then turned her attention back to Ka'ron. After two glasses of Cîroc and cranberry and a few puffs of the hookah, she was feeling herself.

Autumn began to dance in her seat as a combination of Reggae songs played through the speakers. Reggae was her favorite kind of music, and that combined with the alcohol had her feeling herself. Ka'ron watched her with low eyes. He knew that was his homey's sister, but he couldn't deny how cool and undeniably beautiful she was.

"Let's dance." He stood up and grabbed her hand. There was no need to go to the dance floor, so they stood right there and danced. Autumn was impressed; Ka'ron was winding his hips and thrusting to the beat. They were all enjoying themselves until Autumn was getting yanked by her arms. She screamed as she looked up and saw Mason with an angry scowl on his face.

"What the fuck, bruh? Don't be yanking on her like that!" Ka'ron yelled which caused his homeboy to look up and see what was going on.

"Nah, nigga, this my girl, and she being disrespectful as fuck. Got bitches calling me saying my girl with some random ass nigga." Mason was all in Autumn's face.

"Let me go, Mason; damn. Whatever bitch called you, go be up on her. It's obvious she wants you," Autumn explained.

"Look, Autumn." Hannah pointed to the dance floor and saw none other than Katrina. Autumn was sick of her ass. She snatched away from Mason and went to sit back down. She knew Ka'ron wasn't going to let him near her, so she wasn't worried.

"So you just going to sit your ass over there when I'm telling your ass to come on?" he yelled over the music to Autumn. The whole time Katrina was looking and laughing with her friends.

"Look, potna, go on about your business. You can holla at sis when you pipe the fuck down." Ka'ron put his foot down.

"Sis huh? Yeah okay, I got bitches I call sis, and I've fucked them," he said to Ka'ron. Then he looked at Autumn and said, "I'll be by there later," and walked off.

Autumn couldn't believe that he said that shit in front of her friends. She stared at his back until he was gone. She was ready to go, but Ka'ron and Hannah convinced her otherwise.

Once the night was over, everyone went their separate ways. Waiting for Autumn once her and Hannah pulled up to their dorm was none other than Mason. She already had a feeling that he would be waiting on her. He was beside her in two point five seconds when she stepped out of the car.

"Come sit with me in my car so we can talk," Mason demanded.

Autumn hesitated because she knew he was upset. She looked up at Hannah, causing Hannah to ask, "You good?"

"Yeah, she good; she will be up in a minute." Mason grabbed her arm and pulled her to the car. Autumn was moving kind of slow because she was intoxicated.

Once they were in the car, Mason slapped the shit out of her and said, "How dare you embarrass me like that?"

She looked up at him with tears in her eyes. She felt like he embarrassed himself; no one told his ass to come up in there acting stupid because of something that Katrina called and told him. She knew that she and Ka'ron were flirting with each other, but it was innocent. It's not like he caught them fucking or some shit.

"I did not. You ran up in there because of some shit that bitch Katrina told you. Ka'ron is a friend of the family, and he is harmless. You did all of that for nothing," Autumn cried.

"You should have come with me. You are my woman," Mason expressed.

"Not when you're angry. I have to go, Mason." She reached for the door handle, but he locked it fast.

"Listen, Autumn, I'm sorry I hit you, but you were wrong. Maybe I shouldn't have listened to Katrina. I just lose my mind at the thought of someone else touching you." He grabbed her hand which she snatched away at first.

He looked up at her and tried again; this time he kept eye contact with her, and she let him grab her hand. He kissed the back of it and laid his head on the headrest.

"I know a nigga not right sometimes, but I love your ass. I would do anything for you, and you need to know that. But what I won't tolerate is you all up in another nigga's face. You need to cut him off."

"But you don't understand; he has been around since I was a little girl. He is just a family friend. I can't cut him off. He is always around my sister, her boyfriend, and even my grandmother. There is no cutting him off." Autumn tried to get him to understand where she was coming from.

Too bad he didn't at all, and she knew that when he said, "You heard what I said."

Chapter 4

Autumn opened her eyes as her alarm clock sounded. She reached over and pressed the dismiss button on her phone to silence the alarm.

"Damn, Hannah, this is all your fault." She looked over at her roommate who was sitting up stretching her arms up in the air. Autumn did the same as she swung her legs over onto the side of the bed so that she could stand up.

"Uuh uhh, girl. You wanted to go to the hookah lounge just like I did," said Hannah as she stood headed to the bathroom.

That was true; Autumn was complaining about Mason, so Hannah suggested they go out and have some fun. Autumn agreed because she was tired of sitting in the dorm all night.

Autumn laughed as she walked over to her mini fridge and grabbed a bottle of cran-apple juice. She opened it and took a few big gulps before going inside her closet to find something to wear to class.

After picking out a pair of teal skinny jeans and a black fitted tee, she walked into the bathroom once her roommate walked out. Autumn wanted to stay in bed but knew that she couldn't. School was important to her. She only had the rest of this year, plus her senior year, until she got her bachelor's. She planned on getting her master's after that. Autumn had her life mapped out. She would love for Mason to be a part of her future, but if he kept spreading that 'D' and treating her any kind of way, then he wouldn't be.

"Come on before we're late," Autumn told Hannah as she slipped on her Vans. She grabbed her book bag and draped it across her shoulders.

"I'm ready," said Hannah once she had grabbed her bag. Soon after, they were both out the door.

The first person that they saw was Katrina. They gave each other a look before rolling their eyes. Katrina had a smirk on her face as Autumn and Hannah walked by.

"I swear this bitch thinks she is all that," Katrina said loud enough for Autumn to hear.

"Nah, hoe, apparently you think I'm all that," Autumn said with the roll of her eyes as she kept walking. She wasn't with the shits and was seriously tired of this bitch trying her. She felt as if Katrina was trying to say little shit so that Autumn would respond in a way that would get her kicked off the team. But, nah, Autumn wasn't stupid. She knew to catch the hoe off campus.

Autumn and Hannah walked into class and spoke to Professor Thomas as they passed him outside the door.

They sat on the third row, as always, before pulling out their laptop and waiting for class to begin.

English Lit was one of Autumn's favorite classes. Professor Thomas always made class interesting. She loved to write and always aced her papers. If she didn't want to be a teacher, she would become an author, which she thought about doing anyway once she graduated and her career was moving in the right direction.

The hour and a half time slot actually went by fast. She didn't have another class for two hours, so she and Hannah decided to go to the cafeteria to grab a bite to eat. Autumn definitely needed it after the night she had.

As soon as Autumn sat down with her salad, her text message notification went off. She pulled her phone out her pocket and smiled at the message.

Ka'ron: Good morning, Baby Girl.

Autumn: Good morning (smiley face emoji)

Ka'ron: You straight from last night? That nigga didn't put his hands on you, did he?

Autumn: Yeah, I'm good.

Ka'ron: Aight, I didn't like that shit. You ever have problems with that lame ass nigga let me know.

Autumn: Really I'm good. Thanks though, K.

Ka'ron: Have a good day.

Autumn: You too. (Kissy face emoji-peace emoji)

Autumn had the biggest grin on her face when she looked up and caught Hannah staring at her smiling.

"What?" Autumn asked as she prepared her salad to eat.

"And who was that? I know it wasn't Mason, so…"

"It was Ka'ron." Autumn blushed as she took a bite of her salad.

"You like him; I can tell." Hannah smiled.

"No, he is just a family friend. Plus, he looks at me like a little sister."

"Please, Autumn, that man was looking at you like he wanted to eat your pussy." Hannah laughed as she took a bite of her turkey sub.

"Whatever, I have a man anyway," Autumn let her know, which caused Hannah to roll her eyes. She did not like Mason, and it was no secret.

Autumn thought about what Hannah was saying. She did notice Ka'ron licking his lips and looking at her with googly eyes. She smiled again thinking about his fine ass. He was rough around the edges; some may say he was a thug, but she knew him as a sweetheart. She'd known him since she was a little girl and knew him better than most. He was always there for her and her family.

Ka'ron looked like a god. He was brown skinned with light brown eyes. He was six feet five, and his body would make you cream in your panties. He had muscles for days. She remembered him having his shirt off a few times, and she almost fainted. The tattoos that adorned his body were an amazing work of art.

Autumn was brought out of her thoughts by someone sitting beside her. She heard Hannah smack her lips, which made her glance over to see Mason and his homeboy, Quan.

"What's up, baby?" He leaned in for a kiss that she returned.

"Hey," she responded dryly.

She was still upset with him about last night. He demanded that she not be around Ka'ron. That was impossible because he was such a good family friend. She tried to explain that to him, but he wasn't trying to hear it.

"What's up, Hannah? When you going to start showing a nigga some love?" Quan asked Hannah as he took the seat beside her.

Hannah looked up with the stank face and said, "Never, nigga," causing Autumn and Mason to laugh.

"Yeah, you frontin'," he responded while smacking his lips.

Autumn was finished with her salad by now. Mason asked her if she talked to Ka'ron today. Of course, she lied and told him no.

"Good girl," he responded and patted her on her head.

"What the fuck? I'm not a damn dog."

"You my bitch, though." He grinned.

She rolled her eyes and didn't give him the satisfaction by responding. She shook her head and told Hannah to come on. They had class in twenty minutes and needed to get across campus.

"A, when you leave practice, come to my house," Mason said.

"Okay, Mason." She was about to walk off but was pulled back so that he could kiss her once again.

Chapter 5

It was Saturday morning and game day. Autumn lived for game days. She loved the excitement of being on the field looking out at the audience as they screamed for the band and danced in their seat.

Autumn stretched as she stood up to go take care of her personal hygiene. She went ahead and took her shower before Hannah woke up.

When she stepped out the bathroom, Hannah was already up preparing for the day.

"Good morning, girl."

"Good morning," Autumn responded as she sat on her bed and began to apply lotion to her body.

It was only nine o'clock in the morning, meaning they had about three hours before they had to report to the band room. After getting dressed, she decided to call Mason to see if he could take her and Hannah to get some breakfast. Mason may be no good at times, but he would do anything that Autumn asked.

"What's up, baby?" Mason answered the phone groggily.

"Hey, babe, did I wake you?"

"Yeah, but you good; what's going on?" he questioned.

"I was wondering if you wanted to join me and Hannah for some breakfast before we have to head to the band room."

"I can do that. Give me like forty minutes, and I will be there," he responded, and then they said their goodbyes and hung up the phone.

Hannah was walking out of the bathroom when she placed her phone down. Autumn told her that Mason was coming to get them for breakfast. Hannah had no problem with that; she was always down to eat.

As promised, Mason pulled up outside and he called Autumn to let her know that he was outside. Once the two girls were in the car, Mason kissed Autumn before pulling off heading to Midnight Diner.

"You coming to the game, babe?" Autumn turned in her seat and asked.

"You know I'll be there. I never give up the opportunity to see you in that lil' tight spandex outfit," he joked, causing both Autumn and Hannah to laugh.

"You stupid, boy." Autumn shook her head as she continued to laugh.

"Stupid over your ass." Mason glanced over at her and smiled as he pulled into the parking lot of Midnight Diner.

The silly times were what Autumn loved about Mason the most. He kept her laughing, and she needed that sometimes. The stress of school, the band, and all the hating hoes got to her sometimes. She prayed sometimes that Mason wasn't cheating on her. She also prayed that he never put his hands on her again because she really did love him.

******

Autumn and Hannah brought their duffle bags with them to breakfast so that Mason could just drop them off at the band room. The band room was clear across campus. Autumn didn't mind walking, but they had their things with them. That bag got heavy sometimes. Mason got out the car once they'd arrived. He opened the door for both women but stood waiting for Autumn to get out. He backed her against the door when he closed it and kissed her lips.

"I love you, baby." Mason licked his lips before pulling away.

"I love you too." She pulled him back into her embrace. When she let go of his hand, he smoothed out his curly hair before he grabbed her bag out the back seat and handed it to her.

"Thanks," she said as they both caught Katrina's eye at the same time.

Katrina rolled her eyes and smacked her teeth looking like the ghetto chick that she was.

"Hey, Mason." She smiled, making her minion, Jalisa, giggle.

Mason's only reply was kissing Autumn so passionately that it almost made Autumn's knees buckle. Hannah gave Katrina the 'what now, bitch' look, making Katrina stomp off like a big ass kid.

******

The Golden Bulls Football team won against Livingstone thirty-five to twenty-one. The band was celebrating as they marched off the field. Katrina and Autumn led the auxiliary squad off the field as they performed a celebratory march. The band was what the crowd loved to see at games. The band director, Dr. Willie, kept the band's music up-to-date with a little old school incorporated in there as well.

Autumn looked over when she heard her name being screamed. She saw her whole family: Wynter, Summer and her boyfriend, her grandmother, Wynter's husband and kids, and even Ka'ron. She smiled as she continued to perform but also looked around for Mason. When she spotted him, he had a displeased look on his face. At that point, she knew he had seen Ka'Ron, but what was she supposed to do? She told him that he was a family friend.

After getting back to the band room, Autumn got dressed back in her tights and T-shirt before meeting her family outside.

"Hey, Memaw," she spoke and hugged her grandmother first.

"You did a great job out there. Your solo was on point, baby," Memaw congratulated her.

Her solo was only about twenty seconds, but it was the point that she was on the field moving on her own as the rest of the auxiliary squad and dancers stood at attention.

"Thank you so much," she said as she hugged everyone else. Her hug with Ka'ron lasted a little longer than it should have. He kissed her temple just as Mason stepped up. Robert felt the tension and stepped up beside his boy. If his boy was going to have a problem, then so would he.

"What's up, Autumn?" Mason grabbed her around the waist not wanting to show out in front of her family.

"Hey, babe. Everybody this is Mason." She kissed him on the cheek.

"Oh, this is theeee Mason?" Memaw asked, putting emphasis on the.

"This is him in the flesh." Autumn grinned, glancing over at her man.

"How are you all doing today? Did you enjoy my baby's show?" Mason spoke to everyone and put his arm around Autumn to stake his claim.

He glanced over at Ka'ron because he could see the lust in his eyes for Autumn. He wanted to let him know that his girl was definitely off limits. Mason had never really met her family before. They'd been to other games, but he had no desire to meet them and still didn't. He only came over today because he saw Ka'ron.

"Yes, we did," everyone responded in unison.

Memaw wasn't falling for it; she noticed his ass was fake when he first walked up. She didn't like him and prayed that Ka'ron stole her baby's heart. She could tell they had an interest in each other. Matter of fact, every time Ka'ron was around the family, Autumn started blushing.

"Well, Mason, after Autumn freshens up, we are going to Cheddar's if you want to join; Hannah you too," Memaw said as Hannah walked up. They both said that they would and headed to Autumn's dorm.

Chapter 6

"Girl, I'm glad your grandma invited me to eat. I am starving," said Hannah as her and Autumn were getting dressed. Both of them had already showered and were quickly trying to get ready so her family wouldn't have to be downstairs too long.

"You know my family loves you. But why did they invite Mason?" Autumn said as she made the stank face. You know, the one where it looks like someone passed gas, and it stinks like hell. She continued to say, "I know they don't know my feelings for Ka'ron, but damn. For real though, I don't even know how they would feel about me and Ka'ron. He is older than me, and he also has been friends with my sister, Summer, since they were kids. He is also friends with her boyfriend. I don't know. I shouldn't even be thinking about another man because I'm with Mason, right?" She blew out an exaggerated breath as she plopped down on her bed so that she could slip her feet into her shoes.

"Well, it's no secret that I don't really like Mason. Being your friend, I'm going to keep it real with you. Out of all the girls on campus that be messing with you and spreading these so-called rumors about Mason, someone has to be telling the truth; everybody isn't lying on that man. Now, I know the first person you thought about was Katrina. I think something did go down, but he doesn't want her anymore. Just be careful with him. I know you have developed a love for him, but everyone is not worth your love. You know the saying: some people are only around for a season." Hannah stood in front of Autumn so that she could hear and understand everything that she was saying.

******

Everyone was seated and had ordered their food. Mason was sitting to the right of Autumn while Ka'ron was sitting to her left. She knew Ka'ron sat there on purpose, and she could only shake her head. Hannah sat in front of her, giving her the side-eye. Mason was being the perfect gentleman, and she thought that was funny considering he was really an asshole.

"So, how long have you been with my sister, Mason?" Summer asked before she took a sip of her water.

"A little over a year." He looked over at Autumn and smiled. Autumn returned the gesture, and then her eyes fell on Ka'ron, who was shaking his head. He knew this fool was putting on a show and didn't like it one bit. He felt that Autumn could do a whole lot better than this fool.

"Why haven't you ever bought him around when WE…" Ka'ron put emphasis on *we* to make a point before he continued to say, "get together for the holidays and the summer?" He was staring right at Mason.

Mason was becoming upset; matter of fact, he didn't answer Ka'ron. Summer, Wynter, Roman, and Robert wondered what was going on. The only one who had an idea was Maggie, and of course, grandmothers always knew. Autumn gave Ka'ron the eye, silently asking him to behave. Besides, there was nothing between them, and she didn't want Mason to think that it was. That fool seemed crazy.

By that time, the waitress had brought everyone's food and had begun to pass it out. Mason stuck his hand under the table and squeezed the hell out of Autumn's thigh as he leaned over and said, "Keep looking at that nigga and see what's going to happen."

Autumn had tears in her eyes as she looked over at him and wondered what his problem was. She couldn't say anything because he was squeezing so hard. Hannah saw the look on her face and could see Mason's hand. She decided to speak up and hoped that he would stop hurting her friend.

"Mason, when do you all start track practice?" Hannah looked over at him.

It took a few seconds to focus on Hannah and let go of Autumn, but when he did, he said, "Indoor practice has already started."

"Hmm, that's where you go missing to sometimes." Hannah rolled her eyes before picking up her fork to take a bite of her food.

Mason clenched his fists but looked over Hannah's comment. He was trying his best to make a good impression on Autumn's family.

"Oh, track and field is one of my favorite sports. What events?" Robert, Autumn's sister Summer's boyfriend, asked.

"A couple of events actually. The 200 and 100-meter dash and the 4x200-meter relay."

"You know what? I remember seeing you during regionals. Autumn, did you know your man really has talent?" Robert looked at a smiling Autumn and said.

"Yes, I do," she responded happy that the conversation had changed, and he wasn't focused on her anymore. She leaned over and pulled his face to hers before kissing his lips. She wiped the lip gloss off of his lips before eating her food.

The rest of the evening went by smoothly. Every now and then Ka'ron would try to get Autumn's attention, but she wouldn't take the bait. She didn't want to argue or fight with Mason later. She was going over to his house to stay the night and only wanted happy times. After dinner concluded, Autumn said goodbye to her family and left with Mason. After they dropped Hannah off, Mason headed to his apartment off campus.

Neither of them said anything as Autumn went straight to his room and sat on the bed, removed her shoes, and started messing around on her phone. Once Mason walked into the room, he snatched her phone and placed it on the dresser. He sat on the bed, and she waited for the crazy shit to come out of his mouth.

"I'm not going to tell you again to get rid of that nigga. I don't trust him around you," Mason said.

"And I told you that he was a friend of the family, and he wasn't going anywhere." Autumn said matter-of-factly. She didn't know why his ass was acting jealous and shit.

"Look, Autumn, just don't have no personal conversations with that nigga. You my woman, and you know how I feel about that shit," he said as he stood and removed his shirt followed by the rest of his clothing.

"Get out of those clothes and come take a shower with me," Mason demanded, causing her to look up and bite her bottom lip. It's one thing her young mind knew and that was he may be crazy, but he had a nice ass body. Autumn stood up so that she could remove her pants and panties. The whole time she was staring at that 'V' shape leading to his third leg. Mason was blessed, and he knew how to work it. Well, according to her, but Autumn was a virgin when she met him, and she hadn't had any other experience. Once they both were naked, they went to shower. Mason wanted to show her why she didn't need that other nigga in her life.

Chapter 7

Autumn woke up in Mason's bed. She eased out from under him so that she could go relieve herself in the bathroom. After taking care of her business on the toilet, she took care of her hygiene and then walked back to the room to slip on her shorts and T-shirt. She then walked to the kitchen to start breakfast.

Before she pulled the refrigerator open, she went into the cabinet to get her a glass for some water. After getting her glass and a drink of water, she went through the cabinets in search of what she needed. She came across a cabinet that had containers of what looked like protein powder. She knew he worked out a lot so that didn't concern her. What did concern her was what she found as she kept reading the different containers. "Testosterone Heptylate," Autumn said out loud, trying to figure out what it was. She pulled the bottle of pills down to read the label. It wasn't really giving her any idea of what it was, so she grabbed her phone off the counter and googled the prescription name. She knew what testosterone was, but she needed to know why he was using it.

Her eyes stretched wide as she read the content on her phone. She couldn't believe that Mason was taking a performance enhancement drug. All types of things were going through her head. She wondered if he was really as great as he seemed on the track. She wondered if these pills were the reason why his body was so amazing. She knew from TV shows, movies, and news articles about athletes abusing steroids that the drug could make you irritable and angry. She wondered if that's why he raised his hands to her at times and could easily get angry. She had so many questions; the main one being why he felt the need to go this route. She was so deep in what she was doing that she didn't notice him standing there watching her with the pill bottle in her hand.

"You find what you were looking for?" Mason inquired, startling her.

"I… I…" Her mouth opened and closed a few times not knowing what to say.

He walked closer to her and took the pill bottle out of her hand before looking at it and placing it back in the cabinet. He then turned to face her; he looked down and saw what was on her phone.

"Why the fuck you going through my stuff, Autumn?"

"I wasn't; I was about to cook and was looking for everything." She trembled as she saw that look in his eyes. He was angry, and she didn't know what he would do.

He smirked at the fact that she was scared in that moment. She had only seen this particular look once before. She couldn't help but think back to that moment.

About six months ago, Autumn was at a Kappa party with her friends having a good time. They were lit after having a few drinks. One of the Kappas pulled her into his battle dance. He was grinding into her ass, bending her over, and he even picked her up and placed her on his shoulders like he was eating her pussy. The crowd was going wild cheering them on. Autumn was enjoying herself and was laughing when she looked up into the murderous eyes of Mason. She panicked causing the guy to almost drop her. When the Kappa put her down, he gave her a hug not realizing the danger she was in.

Immediately after, she was headed to her friends but got snatched up and dragged out of the party by Mason. She was so embarrassed that she could only hold her head down as her friends tried to save her. Mason finally got Autumn into his truck and headed to his house. The whole ride there was eerily silent. All types of thoughts were going through her head. She didn't know what to think. Once they were inside of Mason's home, he went off.

"How dare you embarrass me like that? Had that nigga dry humping your hoe ass." WHAMP! He went across her face.

"I was just having fun. I'm sorry!" she screamed back at him only to be met with a punch to the chest that knocked the wind out of her and caused her to fall to her knees and hold her chest.

That night after he beat het, he left her right on that floor and didn't return until the next morning. She was in the same spot. He apologized to her as she cried. He felt bad for what he did, but at the same time, he felt she deserved it. He helped her in the tub and catered to her until she forgave him.

Autumn was jarred out of her memory when Mason pushed her against the stove.

"You have no business going through my shit, Autumn. That stuff is personal."

"I'm sorry. I wasn't looking for anything," she said as she backed away from him, causing him to move forward.

"Nobody can know I'm taking this, Autumn. I could be kicked off the team and lose everything," Mason said as he stopped in front of her.

"I… I won't tell anyone. I swear," Autumn said as her back hit the wall.

Mason studied her for what felt like five minutes, but in reality, it was only a few seconds.

"I hope I can trust you. If I lose my shit, then you losing yours."

"What… What do you mean?" Autumn was confused about what he meant. What could he make her possibly lose? The longer they're together, the more things she found wrong with him. She wanted the old Mason back.

"You know what I mean…" He paused for a second and the devious smile on his face made her uncomfortable.

"I know you love to be on that field, baby girl. I would hate to snatch that shit away, but I will," he responded and then had the nerve to try and kiss her on the forehead. Autumn turned her head to the side and placed her hand on his chest. Her eyes were wide because she couldn't believe that Mason would do that.

"I don't know what you thinking. How are you going to threaten me and then try and kiss me? I can't believe you would do something like that to me? You claim you love me but would take something away I love. What? You going to use Katrina to do it?" Autumn said as tears built up in the corner of her eyes.

Mason shrugged his shoulders and said, "You worried about the wrong thing. You need to be worried about not telling anyone my secret."

"I said I wouldn't tell!" Autumn screamed.

Mason's chest rose and fell as he calmed himself down. He had more to say to her ass.

"You make sure you tell that nigga to stay away from you too. I see how he looks at your ass. He wants to fuck you." Mason backed away from her. He sat at the counter and put his face in his hands. He really hoped Autumn didn't tell anyone. His parents would be so ashamed of him.

"I doubt that, Mason. I've known him since I was a kid. I told you that." She relaxed a little since he walked away from her.

"You just don't understand." He shook his head from side to side.

She didn't know what the hell he was talking about, but she was curious. She slowly walked over to him and asked, "Understand what?"

Mason looked up at her with red-rimmed eyes. He pulled her between his legs before he spoke.

"I can't lose you, and I can't lose track. I use those pills to help me win. If I don't win, my parents will be upset with me. It happened once, and they didn't talk to me for weeks. My parents are hard on me. It's been that way since I was a little boy running for AAU."

At this point, Mason had tears falling from his eyes as he silently cried. He knew exactly what he was doing. Judging by Autumn's actions, it was working.

She stepped closer to him, circled her arms around his neck, and said, "Babe, you are awesome. You don't need that stuff. It has bad side effects, and I don't know what I would do if something happened to you. Please stop for me," she said as she lifted Mason's head to look into his bloodshot eyes. She had never seen him like this, so she knew what he told her about his parents really bothered him.

"I know you want your parents' approval, but you have to make sure you are safe, and your health is A1. Please, do this for me." She opened the cabinet, reached inside, and pulled the pills out. She handed them to him which caused him to stare up at her for a minute. He then stood up and walked over to the sink. He opened the bottle and poured them into the garbage disposal before flipping the switch on washing the pills away.

He looked back at Autumn who was smiling from ear to ear and said, "Thank you."

Mason walked over and hugged her. She kissed his lips before telling him, "I love you."

"I love you too," he replied.

Autumn had some errands to run so she got dressed and left. As soon as she was out the door, Mason went into his bedroom and entered his closet. He reached in the very back, pulled out another pill bottle, and opened it to pour two tablets in his hand before returning the bottle to its original hiding spot. He popped the pills in his mouth, swallowed them, and got ready for his day.

Chapter 8

"What? Are you serious right now, baby girl?" Ka'ron asked in disbelief as he and Autumn sat on her grandmother's back porch.

After hearing Mason's story, she decided to stick it out with him. That meant no matter how sexy or cool Ka'ron was, the flirting had to stop.

"I'm sorry, Ka'ron, but I shouldn't be having these feelings for you. I have…" Autumn began but stopped once she realized what she said.

Ka'ron smiled as he looked her over, admiring her, and said, "You feeling me, Autumn?"

This shit was hard enough for her to do, and Ka'ron wasn't making the task any better by openly admiring her. Ka'ron was a strong individual; there was no way he was going to stop showing love to Autumn just because her punk ass insecure nigga wanted it to happen.

"I… I…" Autumn dropped her head in defeat. The cat was out of the bag now. Ka'ron knew how she felt.

"Autumn, look at me. You know I don't like when you look down. Be proud of that shit. I'm a cool ass nigga. Definitely realer than what you dealing with now. I can tell you now, baby girl, that any nigga that will ask you to cut off someone who has been around not only you, but your family, is dangerous. He is jealous, and that shit scares me. Do that nigga be putting his hands on you?" Ka'ron turned his head toward her and raised his eyebrow in a questioning manner.

Autumn didn't say anything, but the look on her face said it all. She wouldn't lie to Ka'ron; she wasn't set up that way. She just hoped he minded his own business.

"Oh hell naw, Autumn, what the fuck? You letting this man hit you?" he said as a look of disbelief crossed his face. He stood up and paced the steps.

"It's not like that, Ka'ron; it was only a few times, but I…"

"Don't you dare blame yourself." He cut her off as he shook his head.

Autumn didn't say anything else because that's exactly what she was going to do; blame herself. Ka'ron knelt down in front of her and wiped the tears that began to fall from down the sides of her face. He could see her fight within about Mason. Either she wasn't sure if she wanted to stay, or he threatened her to stay. Either way, the shit was wrong.

"Listen to me, baby girl. Whatever it is, you don't deserve that. I'm going to grant your wish and leave you alone, but the first time that nigga goes off on you in the future, you have my number. Now, just to let you know,

I'm feeling you too. I'm going to let you get this little puppy love out your system because when he messes up, I'm making my move." Ka'ron expressed his true feelings before reaching up and placing his hand on the back of her head. He pulled her close, placed his lips on hers, and then parted her lips with his tongue. She melted instantly into him not knowing what the feeling was. Her stomach fluttered, and it felt like she was having palpitations in her chest. He pulled back and admired her with her eyes still closed and her mouth formed in an 'O' shape. She looked sexier in that moment with her coils all over her head with some dropping into her forehead.

"Breathe, baby," he smiled and said once he didn't see her chest moving up and down.

As Autumn opened her eyes, her cheeks were flushed red with embarrassment from the way Ka'ron was staring at her. She was so into the kiss that she didn't notice he pulled away. It felt as if his soft lips were still against hers. He licked his lips as he stood up.

"The fuck going on out here?" Robert, Summer's boyfriend, walked outside and asked. He looked between the two and shook his head.

"Why y'all sneaking around?" Robert inquired.

"Man, it ain't nothing to come clean about... yet," Ka'ron admitted as he walked back into the house.

Autumn slumped down in the chair to get herself together before joining the others. She looked up at Robert and shook her head.

"What you shaking your head for, sis? You know my boy feeling you; you also know that other nigga ain't no good for you. I hope you make the right choice." Robert then turned around and went back into the house.

By the time Autumn went back into the house, everyone was headed to the dining room for Sunday dinner. After saying grace, the family dug into the delicious meal that Maggie prepared.

After taking a few bites of her chicken, Autumn placed her hand on Summer's stomach and smiled.

"Only two more months and I get to meet this little guy."

"Yes, and I am so ready. This little thing is very active," Summer expressed as she ate her food.

"My baby is not bothering you." Robert leaned down and kissed Summer's belly.

"Well, maybe your ass should try and carry a baby then," Summer sassed as she rolled her eyes, causing everyone to erupt in laughter.

"Nah, God didn't want it that way," Robert said as he stuck a forkful of macaroni in his mouth.

Summer just looked over at him and shook her head while everyone else continued to laugh. Autumn valued the time she spent with her family. She didn't get to come home a lot during football season because of practice, games, competitions, and all of her homework; she just didn't have the time. Only reason she was able to come to family dinner was because she'd caught up on all of her schoolwork.

By nine o'clock, everyone was packing up to leave. Autumn hugged everyone tight, including Ka'ron, who reminded her to let him know when her weak ass man fucked up again.

Chapter 9

"How is she?" Mason asked concerned about Autumn's sister when he opened the door for her.

"She is okay, but she gave us quite a scare. Someone threw a brick through their bay window. The police think it was kids playing, but I think otherwise," she responded as she walked into his apartment and went straight to his room.

Autumn was just coming back from the hospital seeing about her sister. When Wynter called saying that Summer had to be rushed to the hospital, she didn't know what to think. She was glad she was okay because she didn't know what she would do without her sister. Her sisters and grandmother were all she had.

"What do you mean?" Mason asked as he sat on his bed and picked up his PlayStation 4 controller to save and turn off his game system.

"Well, I think her boyfriend is hiding something, and so does she," Autumn explained as she removed her clothes to prepare for a shower.

"Damn, that's fucked up if it's true," he said as he admired her nakedness.

"You sexy as hell, you know that?" Mason inquired as he pulled her onto his lap, causing her to blush.

"You seem tense. Your sister is okay, so there is nothing to worry about. Let me make you feel better," he expressed before pulling her face toward his and connecting their lips. He kissed her so passionately that her pussy was soaking wet.

Mason had been caring and passionate toward Autumn for the past few weeks. He was catering to her every need. Only thing he needed to do was get these hoes in check. They were really coming out the woodworks now that someone spotted them in the mall spending bands.

"Ohhhhh," Autumn whined as she felt the pressure that he was applying to her clit.

"Can I eat my pussy, baby?" Mason whispered against her neck, which was one of her spots.

Autumn replied, "Yes."

Mason laid back, lifted her up, and then dropped her down on his face. He flicked his tongue over her clit in a fast motion, causing her body to tremble.

"Mmm." Autumn placed her hands firmly on the bed to steady herself as she rode his tongue to oblivion. She was in pure ecstasy as he used his fingers to spread her pussy lips and slide his tongue inside her hole, allowing her to bounce on his face. She sat straight up and caused his nose to tickle her clit. Soon after, she was trembling and raining down on his face.

Autumn fell over on the side of Mason with her eyes closed as she rode the wave. She opened her eyes to a shirtless Mason stepping out of his pants.

"You feeling better, babe?" Mason inquired as he made his way to the edge of the bed. He spread her legs and admired the glistening of her pretty, pink, bare pussy.

"So much better. Now give me that dick," she demanded.

Mason smiled back at her and said, "Oh, you think you running something? Tell me how much you want it." He laid on top of her and commenced to kissing her.

"I want it bad, baby. Please." He watched as her hand traveled down to her pussy. He became angry, smacked her hand away, and said, "What I tell you about that shit?"

Autumn's eyes stretched wide as he stood and yanked her ankle, pulling her to the edge of the bed. He stared at her intensely as he stroked himself. He yanked her up, flipped her over, and then pulled her up so that her feet were planted on the ground.

"I don't know what your ass don't get about not touching my pussy." Mason angrily pushed her back down so that her face was buried in the mattress. He lifted her left leg, placing her foot flat on the bed, before ramming himself into her, bringing tears to her eyes.

"Ahh." Her muffled screams filled the air as he continued to punish her pussy.

Maybe if she was down for this type of treatment, it would feel good. However, he was really angry and taking it out on her. This wasn't what she wanted, and the more she pushed back trying to get him to ease up, the harder he went. Yes, he told her he didn't like her touching herself. She was just playing with him and was trying to entice him to hurry and stick his dick inside of her. Obviously, her plan backfired, and she was feeling it right now.

"Please, Mason, ease up," she spoke once she was able to lift her head.

"Hell nah, this shit feels good as fuck. Damn." He held her waist and rammed into her harder and faster; he was on the brink of an orgasm. Her body betrayed her when she squirted all on his dick. He was right behind her. He smacked her ass and pushed her to climb on the bed, and he was right behind her without pulling out. He continued to grind into her as she whimpered.

"I'm sorry, baby, but you know how I am." Mason kissed up her back and then her neck. His dick hardened back up, and he slowly grinded into her. He pulled out and turned her on her back before entering her again.

"It hurts, Mason. You hurt me," Autumn whimpered.

Calming down a little, he cut her some slack. This time around he was sure to take his time with her. It soon began to feel good to her, and she threw her ass back meeting him stroke for stroke. This wasn't over though. She definitely was going to give him a piece of her mind.

Chapter 10

Mason walked to his closet and reached into the back to pull out his medicine bottle. After grabbing two pills, he closed the bottle and placed it back into its hiding spot. He had an indoor track meet today and wanted to ensure his win. He was going up against one of the best at the indoor facility in Winston-Salem. His parents would be there, and he couldn't risk looking bad in front of them. He knew how they would get if he didn't place, or rather, if he didn't come in first place.

It was 7:30 a.m., and he had everything together for Autumn and him to hit the road. Yes, even after last night, Autumn was going to support her man. She was getting so used to his craziness that it didn't even faze her one bit. He didn't have too many more times to put his hands on her and treat her like shit though.

"Babe, you about ready?" Mason stood at the bathroom door and asked as Autumn was just finishing up with her hair.

"Sure, give me a few minutes to slide my shoes on and grab my bag." She walked up to him and gave him a kiss before walking into the room to grab her big ass purse that she used to pack an overnight bag. Mason's parents got them a hotel room since they knew Mason would need his rest once the track meet was over. After the both of them were sure they had everything they needed, Mason locked up his apartment, and they were on their way to Winston-Salem.

Mason and Autumn arrived in Winston-Salem a little after nine in the morning. After being on the road for over an hour, Autumn was hungry since they didn't eat before they left. She was still tired and didn't understand how Mason was crunk the whole ride. He had Lil' Boosie's album blasting as he bounced in his seat as he rapped every lyric.

"Can we stop and get something to eat? I'm starving," Autumn asked as she turned the radio down a little bit so that he could hear her.

He glanced at his radio before saying, "Yeah, I don't have to be at the facility until eleven thirty. Where you trying to go?"

Autumn's eyes focused out the window to find a place to eat. After spotting a Burger King up the road, she told him, and Mason headed that way.

After pulling off from the drive-thru window, Mason drove to the Marriott Hotel on Cherry Road. They had an hour and a half before he had to get to the facility.

It didn't take long to get to the hotel. After parking the car, Mason grabbed his and Autumn's bags, and then they headed inside the Marriott. Autumn stood to the side as Mason checked in at the front desk. Once he had their room key, they walked to the elevator and then headed to the fourth floor.

Upon entering the room, Autumn plopped down on the bed to finish her breakfast. Mason pulled out a few protein bars and ate them. He stood up and headed to the door when he heard someone knocking.

"Good morning, son," his mother, Rhonda, greeted him as she hugged her son before walking into the room.

"Hello, Autumn," Rhonda said, causing Autumn to look up with a smile and stand to greet her.

"Son, you ready for today?" Terry, Mason's father, asked.

"Yes, sir. It's going to be a great meet," Mason excitedly expressed as he and his father engaged in a man hug.

"It better be, son. Nothing but number one," Terry spoke matter-of-factly. Terry then looked over and spoke to Autumn.

Mason's parents met Autumn at one of his home track meets last year. They both loved Autumn. They could tell that she was very intelligent and had a good head on her shoulders. They thought that she was good for their son.

******

Mason, Autumn, and his parents decided to take one car to the indoor track facility. Once inside, Mason and his family headed to his team's designated area.

"Ahh, Terry. How are you, sir?" Coach Wilson stuck his hand out for Mason's father to shake, and once he shook his hand, the coach moved right along to his mother's.

"Oh, we are great. Just ready to see what my boy here is going to do today," Terry said with confidence as he placed his hand on Mason's shoulder.

"Now, Terry, you know Mason is one of our best; hell, the best."

Tired of listening to his daddy speak, Mason grabbed Autumn and pulled her off to the side.

"Good luck, baby. You got this." Autumn smiled as she grabbed his track jersey and held it tight before standing on her toes in order to give him a few pecks on the lips.

Appreciating his woman believing in him, he gently grabbed her face and kissed her sloppily.

"Thank you. I have to go over here with the team though. Stay with my parents, and I'll see you when the meet is over." Mason bent down to kiss her once more before walking off and standing with his team.

Autumn looked around for his parents because they had already walked off from the coach. She saw Rhonda waving her hand in the air to get her attention, so she walked over and climbed the bleachers to where Mason's parents were sitting.

"I see you and my son are really close now. You're good for him you know." Rhonda genuinely smiled at who she hoped to someday be her daughter-in-law.

"Yeah, well, I used to think so too," Autumn replied.

Rhonda noticed the saddened look on Autumn's face. She was about to ask what she meant, but she heard the gun go off for the women's 100-meter dash. She studied Autumn for a minute, and that's when she saw a dark spot on her face that was obviously covered by makeup. Rhonda was saddened; she thought her son was over hitting women. She remembered that was why his previous girlfriend broke up with him. She just shook her head and observed the events until it was time for Mason to run.

An hour later, Mason had already run the 100-meter dash, taking the first-place spot. Now, he was at the line stretching out for the 200-meter dash.

"Runners on your marks," was heard through the loud speaker commanding that the runners get ready in their blocks.

Mason could be seen in his favorite lane: four. Autumn and Rhonda screamed out his name in unison encouraging him to do his best. Mason heard them and smiled to himself. He was in his zone.

"Set," was the next command given. Mason's feet were in his blocks with his right foot about two inches in front of his left as his bottom lifted in the air. His first finger and thumb were placed shoulder length apart on the ground; he was listening intently to shoot out into the wind.

POW! Mason took off, bringing himself into a standing position as he took long, quick strides to catch up with the sprinters ahead of him. Mason kept his breathing under control as he came around the curve and broke into a full-blown sprint. He heard the cheers and the screams as he saw no one in his peripheral. He got comfortable, which was a mistake. Terry noticed that Mason had relaxed and yelled for his son to pick it up. Rhonda stood to her feet and screamed to the top of her lungs. Her son couldn't lose; if he did, Terry would be upset.

There was only fifty meters left when Mason realized that the runner in lane five had gained on him. The runner in lane five and Mason were neck in neck. Mason was ahead by a neck. It was twenty meters left, and when the two were near the finish line, lane five leaned forward and won by his head crossing over the finish line first.

Mason's chest heaved as he stood with his hands on his knees in disbelief. His dad told him all the time not to let up until after he crossed the finish line. He looked up just in time to see the runner for lane five telling him, "Great job." After shaking his hand, he turned his head to where he knew his family was. He noticed three different expressions: anger, hesitant, and jovial.

Today had been a long day. Mason completed all of his events and then left after the official recordings. Back at the hotel, Mason immediately jumped into the shower and stood underneath the showerhead, letting the water beat down on his body. He knew it was coming; he knew his father was already tripping. He knew that, any minute now, his father would be knocking on his hotel door. Even though he came in first place in two events, his father would look at him as a failure.

Autumn was sitting on the bed once Mason came out of the bathroom. She was grinning because she thought he did well. Every time she saw him in action, she as proud to call him her man.

"What the fuck you smiling for?" Mason boomed as he stopped in front of her with his fist clenched ready for whatever.

"I'm proud of you. I love seeing you out there," Autumn responded tenderly, trying to ease whatever tension it was between them.

"There is nothing to be proud of; did you see what happened in the 200 meters? I fucked up," he snapped before pulling on his boxers and basketball shorts followed by slipping his T-shirt over his head.

"What?! You have got to be kidding me. That was awesome, Mason. So what, you came in second? That shit was close. You'll get him next time." Autumn was so sure that she was causing him to see that he was great. However, the only thing she was proving was that she didn't understand. They just had the conversation about his dad the other night.

"You just don't get it."

"Well, make me get it; you win some, and you lose some. Deal with it," Autumn responded nonchalantly.

The next thing she knew, Mason's fist was headed toward her chest. Autumn's face dropped with a look of surprise. On contact, Autumn's airways were constricted as she struggled to catch her breath; the tears in her eyes confirmed that Mason had messed up once again. As soon as she caught her breath, she went off.

"I'm tired of this shit, Mason. You always talk with your fucking hands. Learn how to use your mouth sometimes," Autumn fussed at him.

"Who the fuck you talking to?" Mason raised his hand and was about to punch her again when there was a knock at the door.

Chapter 11

Autumn's eyes fluttered and were met with a dark room. The only light shining was a thin line of light peeking through the curtains from the moon outside. She pushed Mason gently to be sure that he was asleep. When she was sure, she slipped out the bed and sprang into action. Her things were already packed and by the door because the two made sure everything was set for them to leave in the morning. She was dressed in shorts and a T-shirt. Her headscarf was tight around her head as she slipped into her Nike slides. She tiptoed to the door and picked up her bag once she was against the door. She slowly pulled the door open and slipped out, making sure not to make any noise by pressing her palm against the door until it closed.

It was close to midnight as she approached the registration desk.

"Hi, ma'am, I need a room just for the rest of the night."

"Okay, no problem." The woman tapped the keys on her computer, trying to find a room for Autumn as Autumn continued to look toward the elevator.

"Here we go. It will be $92.26."

Although that was a lot of money for the amount of hours that she would be there, Autumn reluctantly handed over her debit card, and in exchange, she received a room key. Autumn hurriedly walked to the stairwell, not wanting to run into Mason or his parents, and swiftly climbed the stairs to the second floor. Once she was inside of the room, she sighed in relief.

Autumn was sick of Mason putting his hands on her. She needed to teach him a lesson. She was no longer going to stand for the bullshit. She sat on the bed and thought about how she was going to get home. She didn't want to call her sisters and get them involved in her bullshit. Plus, Summer was pregnant, and Wynter had a whole family to be there for. She knew her sisters had no problem with coming to her rescue, but Autumn thought that would be selfish of her. Thinking of the only other person that she knew would come to her rescue, she picked up her cell phone to give him a call.

He didn't answer the first time she called, so Autumn figured he was asleep.

"Shit," she said to herself. She went ahead and pulled off her shoes and turned on the TV before lying down.

Autumn was scrolling down Facebook when her phone rang in her hand. She quickly picked up when she saw that it was Ka'ron.

"Hey," she answered in a low voice, and immediately, he knew something was wrong with her.

"What's up, baby girl? You aight?" he asked genuinely concerned about her well-being.

"No, I need a huge favor. Pleeeeeaaasssseeee," she sang, causing him to chuckle a little.

"What you need? I got you."

"I need you to come get me." She immediately began to cry. Ka'ron could hear her through the phone and knew it had something to do with her punk ass boyfriend.

"I can do that. Where you at, baby girl, and why you crying?" He sat up on his bed and stretched. He then got up to take care of business in the bathroom before getting dressed in gray sweatpants, a T-shirt, and jacket since it was kind of chilly outside this time of night in October.

"Mason punched me in the chest. He was mad on some other shit." Autumn explained what happened, and Ka'ron was livid.

"Man, Autumn, even this nigga's parents are crazy. This the kind of man you want to deal with?"

"I know, but I love him. He didn't always act like this." Autumn sniffed as she wiped her eyes.

Ka'ron's jaw tightened at the fact that she was claiming love for another man when he thought he was the one for her. He decided right then to have a conversation with Maggie and her sisters. If he was going to pursue her, he didn't want to do it behind her family's back. They had always been good to him and even considered him family.

Taking a deep breath, Ka'ron asked, "Where are you?"

There was silence on the phone before Autumn said, "At the Marriott in Winston-Salem."

"What? Where that nigga at, man?"

"I left the room when he was asleep and got another room."

"Text me the address, Autumn. I hope you done with this nigga."

When she didn't say anything, he shook his head knowing that it was going to take some doing to get her away from him. He knew Mason's type. He felt a woman was his property and would do anything to keep her. Ka'ron thought for a minute if Autumn was worth it. He felt she was, so he proceeded to go rescue her.

"I'm leaving out now, Autumn. Make sure you text the info, including the room number. Call downstairs and leave me a key. I don't want to wake you if you are asleep. We will just leave a little after check-out time so we won't run into him."

Don't get it twisted, Ka'ron wasn't scared of Mason or his parents; he was doing that for Autumn.

"Okay. I will," Autumn responded lowly before they hung up the phone and she sent Ka'ron the hotel info.

After she did that, she called downstairs to reserve a key for him before drifting to sleep.

******

Mason reached over to grab Autumn, but all he felt was an empty space. He sat up and looked around, thinking that she was in the bathroom. When he saw that the bathroom door was open and darkness stared back at him, he jumped up and screamed her name. He turned the light on and looked around just to see that her things were gone from the front door. Defeated, he plopped down on the bed and called her phone numerous times with no answer.

"Fuck." He flopped down on the bed and wondered where she could have gone since she rode there with him.

His mother tried to tell him last night that Autumn would get tired of him just like his ex did. After his dad put him down so bad in front of Autumn, his mother pulled him to the side to talk about his issues with hitting women. He knew Autumn opened her mouth or his mother wouldn't have come for him. Not only did Autumn get punched in the chest, but he smacked her a few good times in the mouth for saying anything to his mother.

He now regretted it. He couldn't lose Autumn; there was no way. She kept him calm and on the right path. All of a sudden, he jumped up and bolted for the door, grabbing his room key on the way.

Knocking on his parents' hotel room door, he waited. An angry Terry yanked the door open and wondered who could possibly be at his door this time of night, or rather morning. When he saw his son, his demeanor softened thinking that something could be wrong. In a sense, he was right, but he wasn't in any immediate danger like his father thought.

"What's wrong, son? Is everything okay?" Even though Terry got on him earlier, that was still his son and he loved him. He just wanted his son to be the best which is why he was hard on him. He didn't realize how he and his wife's ways were affecting his son, which is why he never let up. His parent called it tough love.

"Did Autumn come by? We got in a fight, and she's gone."

"No, son, she didn't. She can't be far. Maybe you should let her cool off. Maybe she will come back. You did drive right?"

"Yes, sir, but all of her things are gone."

"Well, go back to your room and try to get some sleep. We can't worry about that right now. You drove, so she can't go far. We will revisit this in the morning."

Mason nodded his head in understanding. He turned around and headed back into his room and tried calling Autumn but got the same results as before: no answer.

Chapter 12

Ka'ron slid the key card in the slot and opened the door once the light turned green indicating that the door was unlocked. He quietly walked in to find Autumn in a deep sleep. Slobber was oozing out of the side of her mouth as she lightly snored. His eyes traveled down to her thick body, which wasn't covered with anything but brown, laced panties and a T-shirt. If he didn't know any better, he would think she fell asleep half-naked on purpose.

He looked down at his watch and realized that it was a little past 2 a.m. He was tired as hell from working all day and then hitting the road. He had just settled in his bed and fell asleep when Autumn interrupted his sleep. It didn't matter though; he'd do anything for her, especially when her life was on the line. She was stranded since she refused to ride back with Mason. He couldn't let her suffer, so there he was.

He pulled his shirt over his head and slipped out of his shoes and sweats before lying on the empty side of the bed. Feeling the bed dip down, Autumn peeked out of one eye, and once she noticed it was Ka'ron, she relaxed. She slid over close to him, causing her ass to touch his thigh. Ka'ron sensed that she needed consoling, so he turned and draped his arm around her waist and nuzzled his face into her neck. After sensually kissing her collarbone, his body relaxed, and he slowly fell asleep.

******

Beep, Beep, Beep. Autumn reached over to grab her phone and pressed the dismiss button to turn the aggravating sound off. She looked to see that Mason had called her numerous times and had sent plenty of text messages. She didn't even bother to read them or return his calls.

She felt Ka'ron stir in his sleep, causing her to place her phone down and turn around facing him. Her hand went to his face as his eyes slowly opened. Autumn smiled and gazed into his eyes. Ka'ron was a handsome man sculpted to perfection. Her hand traveled down his brawny arms.

"Girl, you better stop that shit before you start something you can't finish," Ka'ron expressed with a crooked smile on his face.

Autumn smiled before saying, "Thank you."

"For what, baby girl?" he asked as he pulled her closer to him.

"For coming to my rescue." She laid her head on his shoulder as he pushed a piece of hair back under her scarf.

"You know I got you. I told you that. Now what you gon' do about old boy?"

"I really don't know, Ka'ron," Autumn solemnly said, causing Ka'ron to sit up and making her fall onto the bed.

He stretched and stood up, adjusted his morning wood, and headed to the bathroom.

"I don't understand you, Autumn. That nigga dogs you out, man." He shook his head as he disappeared into the bathroom.

Autumn didn't say anything; she knew he was right, but she didn't want to leave Mason. She was blinded by what she thought was love. Ka'ron hoped she saw the light someday.

She didn't say anything else. She sat her clothes out on the bed and went to take a shower when Ka'ron came out the bathroom.

After thoroughly washing herself, Autumn wrapped a towel around herself and walked into the room. Ka'ron was sitting in the chair by the window and looked her way.

"Maaannn." He shook his head before continuing to say, "Why you come out the bathroom like that when you know I'm pissed at you?" Ka'ron held his dick, which was growing by the second. He was a man who was definitely attracted to her, and there was no way around it.

Autumn didn't say anything. Ka'ron was cool, but she felt he needed to respect her decision whatever it may be because she was undecided right now.

Autumn sat on the bed and grabbed her lotion. The towel fell open a little, and he could see what she was working with between her legs. Ka'ron stood to his feet and slowly walked over to her, never losing eye contact. He reached for her towel and caused it to open all the way. His finger traced her face, down to her collarbone, and then her breast, causing her body to shiver.

"You deserve better, baby girl."

The intensity in his stare caused her to cower. She was feeling things she'd never felt before. She felt like she needed another shower and was embarrassed by it. She didn't want to get up for fear that there was a wet spot underneath her. All she could do was hold her head down, only for him to lift it back up and place a sensual kiss on her full-sized lips.

"You deserve a real nigga; someone that will protect your heart, mind, body, and soul. Someone who will love you the way a queen should be loved. I can be that for you, but not until you ready." He caught the tear that fell from her right eye with his thumb.

"But right now…" He lowered himself down, draped her legs over his shoulders, and then lifted her by her ass up into the air, making sure not to drop her. He walked toward the wall and said, "I'm about to show you what you're missing. Show you how I can handle this body," he spoke confidently, and her body hit the wall with a thud. She stared down at him wide-eyed just as he latched onto her clit.

"Ahhhhhh," she screamed out as he held her in the air by her ass. She didn't know what to do. This nigga had her ass up in the air eating the hell out her pussy. He slurped, bit, and licked every fold and covered every spot.

Autumn held onto his head for balance; although he wasn't going to let her fall. Her body violently shook as she released on his face.

"Damn, you drowning a nigga." He slurped up everything but didn't stop.

Autumn's head went back in pleasure with her back arched as she moaned. Her body released twice more before he finally let up and eased her down. Her legs went around his waist as she tried to reach for his sweatpants. He smacked her hands away while shaking his head side to side.

"Nah, you not ready for that yet." Ka'ron backed up from her and watched as her chest heaved as she tried to catch her breath.

She walked on wobbly legs to the bed and fell back on the cool sheets to get her breathing under control. While she did that, Ka'ron took this time to take a shower himself.

Autumn looked over at the clock and saw that it was almost time to go. She decided to hop in the shower with him to kill time.

"I knew your ass was coming; come on, so I can wash you." Ka'ron smiled as he pulled the shower curtain back for her.

Chapter 13

Mason never did get ahold of Autumn. He was livid that she would pull this bullshit. He was standing in the lobby beside his parents as they checked out. Mason kept looking around in hopes that he would see her walking their way. He had a feeling that she was still in the hotel.

"It will be okay, son; you will see her back at school. When you do, don't put your hands on that girl; that's what's wrong with her now. If she is still mad at you, give her a few days," Rhonda told him.

Of course, the shit she was saying to her son was going in one ear and out the other. However, because he respected his mother, he agreed with her before giving her a hug.

They headed out the door with Terry giving Mason a few words about practicing, exercising, and giving it his all at his next meet.

"I will, Dad. Thanks for the talk." Mason and his father hugged right before they stepped outside.

"What the fuck?" Mason screamed, causing his parents to look over at him in confusion.

"Autumn, Autumn," he bellowed as he made his way over to her and Ka'ron. His parents looked at each other and followed suit.

"Son, stop," Terry called after him.

Autumn stood stunned as Ka'ron threw their bags in the trunk and stood in front of Autumn.

"What are you doing, Autumn?" Mason questioned with a hurt expression on his face.

"Just leave me alone."

Ka'ron turned around to face Autumn. He placed his hand on her shoulder and said, "Get in the car. I will handle this."

Autumn glanced at Mason, his parents, and then back to Ka'ron. She nodded her head and turned to the passenger side door and headed that way.

"So your ass just going to walk away from me? You going to be with this nigga now?" Mason tried to get to her but again was blocked by Ka'ron.

"Homey, you need to back up. I swear I don't want to embarrass you in front of your parents."

"Fuck you, nigga; this my girl. She told you she couldn't be around you anymore," Mason said as his father placed his hand on his son's shoulder.

"She also told you that I have been a friend of the family for over fifteen years. Plus, she woke me up out my sleep last night to come here because you hit her a few times. You get no say. Get the fuck out my face," Ka'ron seethed.

"Mason, you put your hands on her? You know better. I suggest you get in your car and leave now," Terry tried to reason with him. He didn't hear it earlier when his wife said it.

"But, Dad, I don't want her with him. That's my girl, and I don't trust him."

Ka'ron let out a chuckle as Rhonda headed toward Autumn's window. In defense mode, Ka'ron stepped in front of her and said, "With all due respect, I won't let anyone hurt her."

"My wife likes Autumn; she wouldn't do such a thing," Terry said, taking up for his wife.

Ka'ron looked at Rhonda and moved to the side, deciding she wasn't a threat. Rhonda only wanted to check on Autumn. She didn't like what her son was doing or the fact that he hit her.

Ka'ron wasn't with the shits, and he wasn't going to be arguing with that fool. He held his hand up, pivoted on his heel, and headed toward the driver side of the car. Mason broke free of his father and rushed to the car, only to bang on it repeatedly.

Ka'ron looked over at Autumn. "This is what you want?" He chuckled before opening his door and grabbing his gun from under his seat at the same time.

He stepped out, cocked it, and then pointed it at Mason.

"I'm not going to tell you again to get the fuck away from my car."

"Come on, son; it's not worth it. Let's go." Terry tried grabbing his son as his wife cried.

People were stopping to look, but Ka'ron didn't care. He didn't live there and could give two fucks about those people.

Mason stood, breathing heavily, and stared at Autumn through the side mirror. He couldn't wait to get her ass alone. He finally gave up and walked away, followed by his parents.

"She's not worth it, son. If she is hanging around that thug, then she may not be for you." Ka'ron heard and just laughed before getting back in his car and heading toward the highway.

Chapter 14

Mason made it back to Charlotte in record time. He was seething the whole way thinking about Autumn and Ka'ron.

That bitch downright disrespected me. I can't wait to see her ass, he thought.

He pulled up to her dorm, backed into a parking space, and then got out and headed to her room. He hoped that she had made it back already since they left before him.

He knocked on her door only for Hannah to answer.

"Hey, Mason. Autumn isn't here," she said with a perplexed look. She was wondering why she wasn't with him since she knew they left together.

"Shouldn't she be with you?" she questioned.

"Yeah, but things happen," he spat angrily as he turned around and left.

He headed back to his car to sit and wait. He pulled out his phone to call her.

Hello, you've reached Autumn…

Mason hit his steering wheel repeatedly when she wouldn't pick up the phone.

Rachel was walking by, saw him acting a fool, and decided to see what was going on. She tapped on the passenger side door and ducked down so that he could see that it was her. His bloodshot red eyes let her know that whatever was going on with him was serious. He popped the lock, and she sat down in the passenger seat before pulling the door closed.

"You okay, Mason?" she questioned.

Mason sighed before looking over at Rachel and asked, "Why are you women so difficult?" He waited for her answer. He really wanted to know if he was the problem or if the women he dealt with were the problem. It was sad that he couldn't see the issue between him and Autumn.

"What? You having issues with your little girlfriend?" Rachel rolled her eyes and neck like only a true ghetto girl could.

Mason cocked his head to the side and said, "Don't do that, Rach. I really need a friend right now."

Rachel softened her demeanor and stared at him for a second before replying, "I'm sorry. What's going on?"

Mason ran down everything that happened yesterday. He didn't leave anything out, not even the fact that he hit her, and it wasn't the first time. Rachel stared wide-eyed when he got to that part. She never wanted to see that side of him. At that moment, she decided to stop dealing with him because she didn't have time for the shits. His dick wasn't worth being beat.

"What's her problem, Rach?"

Rachel sat there biting the inside of her jaw. She contemplated on what to tell him before she spoke.

"To keep it all the way real, Mason. Autumn didn't do anything to deserve that. She was only praising her man for a job well done. You took out the anger toward your father on her. As far as that guy, if he does want her, I can't tell. She and her family have been around him for a minute. He always comes to the games with her family. Now, I can't say if you drop the ball they won't start messing around, but from what I can see, right now they are only friends. Maybe you are paranoid because you do your dirt. Stop putting your hands on her, or you will lose her for good if you haven't already. Shit, 'cause I would have left your ass the first time. That girl must really love your ass," Rachel finished.

The car was silent for a few minutes with each of them in their own thoughts. Mason watched all the cars coming in still hoping to catch Autumn.

"I don't know what's wrong with me. I don't want to hit her, but I get so angry sometimes," Mason said more so to himself.

"It's taking me a lot to say this considering we've been fucking for a minute, but how do you expect to keep her when you hit her and go around cheating on her every chance you get? From what I know, Autumn isn't dumb. She knows about you cheating; she just hopes you change. I got to go. I'll see you around." Rachel opened the door, stepped out, and adjusted her jeans before closing the door and walking off.

Mason picked up his phone once more and still didn't get an answer. He decided to leave a message in hopes that she would call him back.

"Hey, Autumn. I'm really sorry about the way I acted this weekend. I realize that I was taking my anger against my father out on you. I realize my mistakes and will never take my issues out on you. I love you, Autumn. I need you. Please call me back." He pressed the pound key indicating that he was finished with his message and then pressed two to send with urgent delivery. He cranked his car up and headed to his apartment after realizing that Autumn wasn't coming.

******

"Hello," Autumn answered her phone when she saw Hannah was calling. She was monitoring her calls because she was tired of Mason calling.

"Hey, girl. Is everything okay? Mason just came by," Hannah told her.

"See, Ka'ron, I told you he was going to go there," she said to him before giving her attention back to her friend. "That nigga came in second place and spazzed out on me. I left when he went to sleep and called Ka'ron to get me. It was a mess..." Autumn ran down everything that happened, including what went down in the parking lot of the hotel.

"Damn, Autumn, I'm sorry. You okay though, right?"

"Yes, I'm going to stay with Ka'ron tonight. I will see you in class in the morning."

"Okay. Call me if you need me, sis," Hannah said before they hung up the phone.

Autumn laid back on the couch with her feet propped up on Ka'ron.

"I really appreciate you, Ka'ron. It feels good to have somebody there for you when you need them, you know?"

"Yeah, I feel ya."

Autumn had a feeling that Mason would go straight to her dorm. She didn't want to argue with him, so she asked Ka'ron if she could spend the night. Deep down, she knew she was going to give Mason a chance to get himself together. She felt that if you loved someone then you should fight for them. Which may be true, but the only thing she had to realize was that you had to love and fight for the right person, not someone who really wasn't meant to be in your life for a lifetime.

"You know, baby girl, sometimes in life you have to go through the bullshit to know what's real. When real is staring you in the face, you have to grab it before it's not available to you anymore," Ka'ron expressed, letting her know in so many words that he wasn't going to wait forever. He wanted to be with Autumn, but only when she was ready. In the meantime, he wasn't going to stop living his life, and he hoped she realized who was really in her corner.

"How is school going?" He grabbed Autumn's feet and began to massage them.

"Mmm. School is great. I'm passing all my classes, of course."

"That's good. You know I'm going to be front and center at your graduation screaming your name." Ka'ron smiled as he looked over at the faces she was making.

"I know you will."

Ka'ron continued to massage her feet until they decided to order some wings from Wingstop. They talked about life all night long until they fell asleep.

Autumn was so confused. She loved Mason and wanted it to work, but Ka'ron was making his way into her heart. She loved the way Ka'ron treated her like she was the only one that mattered. It didn't help that he ate the hell out her pussy either.

Chapter 15

Autumn woke up bright and early to get ready for class. She enjoyed herself with Ka'ron, but she had to go. She had already showered and was standing in his mirror trying to do something with all her wild hair. After messing with it for five minutes, she finally got it up into a bun at the top of her head.

"You know I love all of this thick hair; it's natural just like your beauty." Ka'ron stepped behind her as he admired her through the mirror.

He then stepped to the side in front of the toilet and relieved himself. He didn't care that she was standing there; that's how comfortable he was with her. He even let out a little poot at the end of his piss. She looked over at him and covered her nose.

"I can't believe you just did that; oh my god," she shrieked as she stomped her foot and stormed out of the bathroom with her eyes wide with surprise.

After Ka'ron washed his hands, he walked out the bathroom laughing as he said, "Ain't no shame in my game, baby girl. We going to end up together sharing more things than that. Get used to it."

Autumn just shook her head at this fool, but she knew that he was serious about wanting to be with her. She slipped her Vans on her feet and waited for him to get dressed. She looked down at her phone at more missed calls from Mason. She just didn't get Mason; he would get angry and hit her at any moment, but he was sitting here calling her nonstop.

"Hey, let me ask you something." Autumn turned around to Ka'ron.

"What's up? You can ask me anything."

"What effect can steroids have on athletes if abused?"

Ka'ron stopped what he was doing and turned to give Autumn his undivided attention. He asked, "Is that nigga on steroids?"

"Just answer the question please."

"That shit is dangerous if abused. If someone is taking too many, then it can throw their hormones off. It can even make some people violent and paranoid."

Autumn sat quietly for a minute thinking about what Ka'ron said. She did her research but wanted to get another opinion before jumping to conclusions. Now she had a feeling that Mason was still taking those damn pills. Ka'ron gazed at her as a tear slipped out her eye followed by more. He walked closer to her and knelt in front of her.

"What's wrong, baby girl?" he asked as he tried to wipe her face free of tears, but they just kept coming. At that point, he got up and sat next to her, pulling her into his embrace and consoling her until she was ready to talk. His right hand moved up and down her back as her shoulders heaved up and down. Another five minutes passed before she finally calmed down. He pulled back and wiped her face.

"One day I was in his kitchen. Long story short, I found a cabinet with some pills in it. They were steroids. He caught me looking and got mad; you know what happened next. After he hit me, he went on this whole thing saying how he has to win, or his dad would scold him. His mom does it too but not as bad. He said he takes them to help him win. I made him promise to stop, and he got rid of them. After this weekend, I think maybe he had more. But, Ka'ron, please don't get mad at what I'm about to say," Autumn pleaded. He promised that he wouldn't and encouraged her to continue.

"I really love him. He wasn't like this at the beginning of our relationship; I swear he wasn't." The look on her face told Ka'ron that she was both disappointed and hurt.

He took a deep breath and thought about what he was going to say. He didn't want her with him at all. He wanted Autumn to come to her senses.

"Look, baby girl, that shit could get dangerous if he can't control it. It would hurt my heart if something happened to you." He paused for a minute to gather his thoughts.

"I understand that you think you love him," he said, putting emphasis on think, "but you have to figure out if all that he put you through is worth it. Just be smart. If you feel like you about to be in a situation, call me, and I will break that muthafucka's legs so that he can't run." Ka'ron looked up at the shocked expression on her face. He chuckled because she hadn't ever seen that side of him.

"I understand. I'm not sure where we stand right now, but I know we need to have a conversation. I'm just going to let him cool off first, and then maybe he and I can talk with a clear head."

Ka'ron was already shaking his head from left to right. He didn't agree with what she was saying but knew he couldn't stop her. He stood up before he said, "Just remember that, if you ever need me, let me know, and I'm dropping everything for you. Let's go before you are late for class. Your ass only has one more year to graduate."

******

Autumn and Hannah were walking out of class when Autumn ran into someone, which caused her books to fall out of her hands.

"I'm sorry about…" Autumn looked up and stopped mid-sentence.

"Watch where the fuck you going, Autumn," Katrina shouted.

Hannah looked at Katrina with the stink face about to give her a piece of her mind when Autumn spoke up.

"Bitch, you watch where the fuck you going. I'm tired of you bitches coming at me just because you want Mason. Well, you can have his ass."

"Really, Autumn?"

Autumn heard and immediately turned around to see Mason. She was kind of scared, so she grabbed Hannah's hand and they took off running. She didn't want to feel his wrath for what he heard her say.

Autumn and Hannah ran all the way to the student union two buildings down while occasionally looking over their shoulder. Autumn knew Mason could catch her if he wanted too, but instead, he stood outside the building screaming her name. When she looked back before entering the student union building, she saw Katrina with her hand on his bicep as she laughed. Mason didn't look happy, but she wasn't worried about that right now; she just didn't want to talk to him right now.

"Bitch, you got me running like I'm on the track team. Got me all out of breath and shit." Hannah stopped, putting her hands on her knees to catch her breath.

"Girl, shut up. That nigga is crazy, and I'm not dealing with him right now; come on."

They both began to walk again until they got in line to grab them some breakfast. Once their tray was in their hands, they found a table.

"What are you going to do about Mason?" Hannah asked as she stirred her strawberries into her oatmeal.

Autumn stirred her blueberries in hers before she said, "To be real with you, Hannah, I love Mason. I just hate his ways. I'm not trying to make excuses for his actions, but he has really been going through something lately. He has a problem that he needs help with. I think that if I help him, he will be okay," she finished and put a spoonful of her food into her mouth.

"It sounds like you are making excuses, Autumn. Everybody isn't meant to be in your life. Some relationships are a lesson. Mason sounds like he is just that. Now that Ka'ron, that's the man for you; I don't care what you say," Hannah said matter-of-factly as she giggled. She observed the look on Autumn's face before her eyes got big, and she gasped before she asked, "Give me the tea, girl."

"What tea?" Autumn questioned although she knew what her friend was talking about.

"Girl, I've known you for years and have been your roommate for two years. I know when you are hiding something, so spill it, bitch." Hannah had the most serious look on her face which caused Autumn to laugh.

"Okay, bitch, damn." Autumn sat up and turned her neck to her left, right, and behind her to make sure no one was looking or listening to her. She then said, "Ka'ron ate the hell out of my pussy, girl. That nigga had me up on the wall with my legs wrapped around his shoulders." Autumn shivered just thinking about it.

"Oh my god, I can't believe you tried to keep that from me. So I take it that it was good," Hannah said as she picked up her orange juice taking a sip.

"Good, nah, it was impressive. He was doing shit with his tongue that Mason never did. He almost had me leaving Mason for real. Then, he ruined it all because I craved him after that, but he said I wasn't ready. My ass had to take a cold shower to cool off."

Hannah burst out laughing listening to her best friend and caused Autumn to laugh as well.

"Hey, Autumn, can I talk to you for a minute?"

Someone walked up and stood beside them, causing both Hannah and Autumn to stop talking and look up. Neither of them knew her, and the way their faces contorted said just that.

"Who are you?" Autumn asked with a mean mug on her face.

"You may not know me, but I'm a friend of Mason's; Rachel," she said, which caused Hannah to smack her teeth and Autumn to roll her eyes. They were thinking that she was coming to tell her that she was fucking Mason.

"It's not like that. I come in peace—"

"What's up then?" Autumn cut her off.

"Look, I spoke with Mason, and he is sorry for what he did. He really loves you. He was damn near crying when he was talking to me yesterday," Rachel said.

Autumn and Hannah burst out laughing, not believing this shit.

"Bitch, your name is one of the ones circulating with the other hoes fucking my man, and you have the audacity to bring your mediocre looking ass over here to try and convince me that this nigga loves me. Did he put your simple-minded ass up to this?" Autumn stood to her feet and faced Rachel.

"He didn't tell me to do shit. I was helping your ass out. Forgive me for me wanting you guys to work. I get it though; if he beat my ass, I wouldn't want anything to do with him either." Rachel flipped her hair over her shoulder thinking she did something. Having enough, Autumn pushed her down, causing her to fall.

"That's for thinking you a slick bitch." Autumn and Hannah grabbed their trays and walked away, leaving Rachel on the floor like the fool she was.

Chapter 16

Autumn went about her day going to the rest of her classes or what not. She was coming out of her last class when she ran right into Dr. Willie, the band instructor

"Autumn, just the person I wanted to see," Dr. Willie spoke.

Autumn smiled and stepped closer to him before saying, "Hey, Dr. Willie, what can I do for you?"

"Let's walk over to this office so that I can show you something," he said and then turned around to walk off with Autumn following him. She didn't know what was going on as her palms became sweaty.

Dr. Willie asked his colleague to borrow his office ahead of time since he knew where Autumn's class was. As soon as they walked in the office, Dr. Willie shut the door and asked Autumn to have a seat before he walked around the desk to sit in front of the computer. After pressing a few keys, he turned the computer screen around so that she could view the video that he wanted her to see.

Autumn's eyes were stretched wide, and her mouth was wide open. She looked up at Dr. Willie and back at the computer screen just as it showed her push Rachel down to the ground. Her face turned red as she looked back up at the band director.

"I…" she began, but there was nothing that she could really say.

"I don't know what happened, and frankly, I do not care. You know the rules to stay in the band." Dr. Willie looked down on Autumn, who was gazing back at him in a daze.

"I just lost it. You know I'm not the type of person that goes around acting this way."

"And that is why this is going to be a warning, Ms. Hart. But next time, you may want to remove yourself from the situation. I'm sure that whatever it was isn't worth you losing it all."

"No, sir, it was not," Autumn sighed.

Dr. Willie then stood up and escorted Autumn back out of the office and wished her a great day.

Autumn was walking to her dorm thinking about who could have done this to her. She searched her mental and didn't remember seeing anyone in the student union that would do this. She didn't see Katrina or any of the other hoes who hated her. Whoever it was did a good job of hiding.

Chapter 17

"Hey, Memaw," Ka'ron greeted her with a hug before stepping into the house and shutting the door.

"Hey, baby, what brings you by today?" Maggie countered as they walked into the kitchen where she was fixing herself leftovers from the day before.

"Dang, Memaw, I have to have a reason to visit you now?"

"Not at all, baby." She placed her hands on her small hips before she said, "But I can see the worry lines on your forehead, boy; don't play with me," Maggie stated matter-of-factly, causing Ka'ron to laugh."

"You're right. I swear we can't get anything past you," Ka'ron said and then slid his hand over his face before sitting in a chair at the kitchen table.

"Before we start, you want something to eat?" Maggie questioned as she put her plate of liver and rice in the microwave.

"No, ma'am, you know I don't eat liver, but can I get some of your famous Kool-Aid if you have any?"

"Sure, baby." She poured him a glass of Kool-Aid and handed it to him before retrieving her plate from the microwave and sitting down in front of him.

"Now, tell me what's on your mind." Maggie picked up a forkful of rice and blew on it before putting it in her mouth to eat it.

"It's Autumn; I keep telling myself that I need to talk to you. I finally got the guts to do it." Ka'ron looked up at Maggie to see her smiling.

"What you over there smiling for?" he questioned curiously.

"Because I know you like her. I see the way you look at her, and I see y'all sneaking and going on to get private time."

Ka'ron's eyes bucked as he listened to Maggie speak. He nodded his head up and down and replied, "I really do, but her boyfriend is in the way. He's not good for her, but no matter what I say, she won't listen."

Maggie placed her fork down and held a stern look on her face and asked, "Why do you say he isn't good for her? I'm asking because I got that same vibe that day at the game when she introduced us."

Ka'ron sat back and thought about what he should say. He really didn't want to tell Maggie everything, but he knew he couldn't keep anything from her. He needed Maggie to trust him.

"Man, Memaw excuse my language, but this muthafucka be hitting on her. He gave her a sorry ass excuse about why he takes steroids. I had to drive all the way to Winston-Salem the other day because they got into it."

Shaking her head from side to side, Maggie pushed her plate away from her because she was finished eating her lunch. She stared at Ka'ron for a minute before saying, "And you mean to tell me that you didn't whip his ass?"

"Man, she didn't want me to. She was already upset, and I didn't want to upset her even more."

"What is wrong with that child? How bad is it?" Maggie asked.

"From what she says, it's one step away from being a real problem. But to me, it's already a problem. She deserves so much more," Ka'ron said and then gulped down the rest of his Kool-Aid.

Ka'ron exhaled to get his anger under control. He didn't know what to do. He wanted to beat Mason's ass. He wanted him to feel the way Autumn felt every time he put his hands on her. He didn't think he would be able to hold back if Autumn came to him again saying that he flipped out on her.

"I knew I didn't like that guy when we all went out to eat. His just didn't give off good vibes. I have to talk to that girl about this."

"No, Memaw, please don't. She won't trust me. I came to you today to get your blessing to pursue her the way I want. Trust me, when I lay my mark, she won't be thinking about him."

Maggie placed her elbows on the table, laid her face on the side of her hands, and observed his demeanor. She could see that he was serious about her granddaughter. His eyes told it all; he loved her. His feelings were way past the "like" stage.

"You know, the only thing I question is the age difference. However, I know that the heart wants what the heart wants. I know you are a good man and will do right by her. I will be more than happy to have you as my grandson-in-law." Maggie's smile was bright as Ka'ron stood to hug her.

"Don't get too ahead of yourself now. I have to get her and date her before we talk about me being an official part of the family." He let go of her and stood there.

"Oh please, I can already see it. She will come to her senses. Watch what I tell you." Maggie stood and lifted her plate and their glasses to take them to the sink. She turned on the water, grabbed the dish detergent, and quickly washed them before placing them into the dish rack to dry.

"I'm so glad you are allowing me to get my woman. Do you need anything before I leave?"

"No, I'm fine. I'm about to go in here and catch up on my favorite shows: *Empire* and *If Loving You is Wrong*."

Maggie reached up to kiss his cheek before saying, "This conversation will stay here as long as he doesn't hurt my baby again. Don't let it happen, Ka'ron; you don't want to catch these hands along with that psycho."

Ka'ron burst out laughing. "You would beat me, Memaw?"

"Damn right," she said, punching him softly in his stomach.

"Ooomph," Ka'ron joked as he said, "Okay, tough woman. But don't worry, he gon' catch it from me if he does. I'll see you later." They said their goodbyes before he headed out the door.

******

It was two days before Mason was finally able to catch up with Autumn. By this time, he had calmed down. He thought about everything his mother, father, and Rachel said. The only person who tried to get him to leave her alone was Katrina. He fucked up when he had sex with her the day Autumn ran from him. Now, she popped up on him every damn where.

Mason was sitting on Autumn's bed while she finished up her homework with Hannah. Hannah kept shaking her head and wished that her friend would leave this trash ass nigga alone. She was confident that this relationship would be over one day though. As soon as Autumn reached her breaking point.

"That's it, thank God." Autumn and Hannah closed their books at the same time.

"Don't you have somewhere to go?" Mason asked Hannah.

"Actually, I don't," Hannah responded as she got comfortable on her bed. There was no way she was leaving her friend alone with him. Whatever he had to say, he was going to have to say it in front of her too.

Mason narrowed his eyes at her and tried to make her back down, but she wasn't having it. She grabbed the remote and turned the television on.

"What is it you want to say, Mason?" Autumn asked.

Mason turned his attention back to Autumn and said, "I'm so sorry for hitting you. I realized by hitting you that you can't tell that I love you."

Hannah smacked her lips, causing Mason to look at her with the death stare. Hannah didn't care because, if it came to it, they would jump his ass.

"Anyway, please forgive me. Just give me one more chance, baby," he pleaded with her.

Autumn sat there staring at Mason; she didn't know whether to believe him or not. Then she thought about Ka'ron. He would probably be the better choice, but she didn't really want to start over. She loved Mason; she really did.

Both Mason and Hannah could see her tossing her answer back and forth from the expressions on her face. Autumn was trying to find a reason to say no. Although all the reasons were there, she decided to give in to love. She smiled brightly, which caused Mason to smile and Hannah to frown.

"One more chance, Mason; that is all. But first, do you know who recorded me pushing Rachel to the ground?

"What?" both Hannah and Mason responded at the same time.

"Why did you push Rachel?" Mason asked.

"'Cause that bitch walked up on her trying to speak on you like her opinion matters. Shit, for all we know, the rumors are true, and you fucked her." Hannah rolled her neck and pointed her finger in Mason's face.

"Nah, but I did run into her when we came back from Winston-Salem. I vented a little, but that didn't give her a right to walk up on you. As far as a recording, I honestly didn't know anything about that."

After he explained his side, they believed him about the recording. As far as him fucking Rachel, he didn't really respond to that, leading Autumn to believe what she wanted.

"Another thing, Mason, if I hear one more thing about you cheating, I'm done."

All Mason could think about was the fact that he just fucked Katrina a few days ago. He hoped she kept her mouth closed.

Chapter 18

Autumn was at her sister's house since no one wanted her to be alone this close to delivery, especially after someone threw a brick through her window.

"Uhhhh," Summer groaned.

"What's wrong? You okay?"

"Yeah, I'm good, sis."

Autumn stared at her sister for a minute, knowing that she was lying. Right when she was about to say something, Robert, Summer's boyfriend, came through the door and greeted everyone. After grabbing her things, she was out the door.

Her phone beeped as soon as she got in the car. She read the message from Mason and smiled. He had been doing good the last couple of days, and she hoped he would keep it up. She put her car in drive and drove around the driveway before pulling onto the street. She picked up her phone when it rang.

"Hey, sexy," Ka'ron said when she picked up.

"Hey." She giggled like a schoolgirl. She hated talking to him sometimes because she got that giddy feeling in the pit of her stomach.

"What you up to, baby girl?" he inquired and then waited for her response.

"Wait, hold on; Robert is calling," she said before clicking over.

"What's up, bro?"

"Autumn, did you know that Summer was having contractions…" Robert began frantically.

"Ahhh," Summer screamed as Robert was talking to Autumn,

"She didn't tell me. I'm on my way back."

"Hurry up," he screamed before hanging up the phone.

Autumn clicked back over to Ka'ron. "Oh my gosh, Summer is in labor. I'm on my way back to her house," Autumn spoke as she desperately busted a U-turn in the middle of the street.

"I will meet y'all there. University, right?" Ka'ron asked.

"Yes," she said and then hung up as she pulled into the driveway. She hopped out her car and ran into the house. Robert instructed her to grab Summer's baby bag while he helped her to the car. Once Autumn slid into the backseat, Robert raced to the hospital.

"Autumn, get in contact with Dr. Armstrong, and let her know we are on the way," Robert said as he drove.

Moans of discomfort filled the car until they reached the hospital. Pulling up to the emergency door, Robert hopped out and got help. Autumn parked the car while Robert went with Summer inside.

******

Hours later, once the family got word that Summer did indeed give birth, Autumn and Wynter headed to Summer's room together. Autumn and her sister, Wynter, walked off the elevator to see their grandma having a conversation with an unknown lady. They heard the lady congratulate her on her great-grandbaby and their grandma asked if whoever was at the hospital with the unknown lady had her baby yet. Autumn and Wynter looked at each other knowingly before walking over to the two. When the lady walked away, they immediately began asking their grandma questions.

After finding out who the woman was, they were livid. They knew their sister thought that Robert was cheating, but a baby? This only caused Autumn to think about Mason and the fact that he constantly cheated on her. She made the decision right then that if she even heard about Mason cheating, she was really done. Whatever he wanted to do to her at that point, she would deal with it or have Ka'ron deal with him because she knew he would.

After promising that neither she nor Wynter would say anything to Robert or Summer, they entered the room to meet their nephew: baby Robert.

"He is so precious, oh my god," Autumn said as she walked close to the bed. She gave Robert the eye but didn't say anything. Ka'ron walked in the room and spoke to everybody. After marveling over the baby for a while, there was a ruckus in the hallway which caused Ka'ron to turn right back around. Nobody knew what to do, Autumn was looking around the room at everyone else. She walked to the door to peer out and yelled, "Oh my god, they are fighting."

Once everything was said and done, her sister, Summer, found out about her boyfriend's

other baby. She consoled her sister the best way she could.

"Wow, that was crazy," Autumn said to Ka'ron as they left the hospital.

"Yeah, it was. That nigga crazy; enough about that though. How you doing?"

"I'm good, how about you?" She gripped his arm as they were leaving the hospital.

"You go back to that nigga yet?" Ka'ron asked, looking down at her.

The cool crisp air hit Autumn's face as they stepped outside. She glared at him as the smile that was on her face dropped.

"Ka'ron, we…"

"Nah, it's okay. Don't even answer." He angrily let go of her and continued to his car. He got inside, not even bothering to open her door.

The ride to Autumn's dorm was a quiet one. Since it was late, he decided to pick up her car from Summer's house the next day. It was almost awkward the way they were acting toward each other in that moment. Autumn kept stealing glances at his handsome face. She didn't want him to be mad at her, but she couldn't help who she loved.

"You know, one day you are going to wish you made a different choice. I want you, Autumn, and I know I can treat you better. I know you tired of hearing it, so this will be the last time you hear me saying it."

Ka'ron pulled up to Autumn's dorm and parked the car as he picked up his phone. He typed something and then turned to Autumn and said, "Have a good rest of your day."

Autumn turned toward him and told him that she would see him later. Autumn stepped out the car just as a girl walked up smiling from ear to ear. The girl was gorgeous. She had brown pretty skin, a thin waist, and a fat ass with a short haircut that fit her face perfectly. She watched as Ka'ron stepped out of the car, grabbed the girl by her waist, and pulled her in for a hug. Autumn frowned and wondered who the fuck she was. She was definitely feeling a hint of jealousy right now. When

Ka'ron turned toward her, he kissed the girl on her neck, causing the girl to giggle. Autumn stomped off like a little girl, making Ka'ron smile.

"You did good, girl," Ka'ron said to his homeboy's sister.

"Yeah, she was big mad." They both laughed as they got in the car so he could take her to work. She was a bartender at a bar in the downtown area.

Chapter 19

Autumn was fuming when she walked into her room. She threw her purse on the bed and paced the floor. Yes, she had a man and hadn't been receptive to Ka'ron's advances, but to throw some girl in her face, she couldn't believe his ass. She walked over to the window and pulled the curtains back just in time to see them pulling off.

Hannah watched Autumn go through different emotions in a matter of seconds. She assumed that it had something to do with Mason.

"Girl, why are you over there acting crazy and shit, what Mason do?"

"This is not even about Mason. Ka'ron tried me. Oh, my sister had her baby. That's a story for another day though," Autumn replied to Hannah.

"Congratulations, boo. Now tell me what Ka'ron said that got you all out of whack?" Hannah swung her legs over the side of her bed and closed her notebook. She wanted to give her friend her undivided attention.

"This nigga just said some shit to me basically saying that if I wanted to be with Mason then do that. Then, he had the nerve to drop me off and pick up some slut that goes here. He was all up on her like she mattered. She was keekeeing like shit was funny." She finally stopped talking and plopped down on her bed.

Hannah burst into laughter and shook her head before saying, "Girl, you are something else." She continued to giggle.

"What?" Autumn questioned with a straight face like she didn't know she was tripping.

"Why your ass trying to play like you don't know? That nigga been trying to get at you for I don't know how long. You can't get mad at him for moving on. What you want him to do? Wait on you while you still play around with Mason? Girl, you tripping for real." Hannah rolled her eyes while smacking her teeth.

"He didn't have to do that shit in my face though," Autumn stated seriously.

Autumn picked up her phone and dialed his number. The first time there was no answer. The second time he picked up the phone laughing.

"Hello."

"Hello, my ass, how you just going to disrespect me like that?" she questioned.

Ka'ron looked over at Danesha and shook his head while mouthing, "She's jealous."

"Baby girl, I didn't disrespect you. You have a man that you supposedly love. I don't have time for the games. You know how I feel, and you choose to ignore it. A, I need to call you back though. I will holla at you." He hung up the phone.

"This nigga just hung up on me." Autumn looked down at her phone in disbelief. She was pouting like she lost her best friend.

Hannah looked at her with sympathy before saying, "Look, babe, if you want him, just get rid of Mason. I know it's easier said than done, but I know you really want Ka'ron but are staying with Mason because that's what you're used to.

Autumn heard everything that Hannah said. She wanted to get her grandma's opinion though, because she always knew what's good for her. She dialed her number and waited for Maggie to pick up.

"Hey, Memaw," Autumn said sadly.

"Hey, baby. What's wrong? You don't sound like yourself."

"Memaw, I have been kind of talking to Ka'ron, but he just pissed me off. I don't know what to do."

"I know; he came by here one day and told me how he wanted to pursue you," Meggie responded.

"He did?" Autumn questioned as her grandma's words brought a smile back to her face.

"He did. Now what that nigga do to you so I can whip his ass."

Autumn told her grandma everything that happened from the time they left the hospital. She also told her how she was having second thoughts about Mason but wasn't really ready to let him go.

"Well, you can't really be upset with Ka'ron, baby. He has told you who he wants. He probably thinks you don't want him. It's up to you if you want to stay with someone who you obviously don't want. Be smart about this. Is this Mason guy worth it? Let me say this. Mason doesn't give me good vibes. I don't know what it is, but he must be fooling you because he is not a nice guy."

"I hear you, Memaw. Looks like I have a lot to think about." She sighed.

"Yes, you do. Now, I just got home from that hospital. I'm about to take a shower and hit the sack."

"Okay, Memaw. I love you."

"Love you too."

They hung up the phone. Autumn looked over at Hannah and said, "She said the same things you said. She also said she doesn't trust Mason."

"Told you. And grandmas know best," was all she said before heading to the bathroom.

Autumn was about to get comfortable until Mason called for her to go downstairs to go get something to eat.

It was almost nine o'clock at night, and she really didn't want to go anywhere but decided to go anyway since she hadn't eaten anything in hours.

******

"Mmm, this is so good. I haven't had pizza in a long time," Autumn expressed as she took a bite of her supreme pizza. Her and Mason were sitting inside the Pizza Hut on Freedom Drive enjoying their meal.

"Yeah, these lemon pepper wings are fire," Mason responded.

They were eating in silence for the most part, only saying little things to each other here and there. Mason didn't want to say the wrong thing while Autumn was contemplating on saying the right thing and letting him go. Every time she played with it, she thought about him getting her kicked off the team. She was so confused.

When they finished eating, Mason paid the tab, grabbed Autumn's hand, and left the building.

"You look nice today, Autumn." He admired her as he stopped on the passenger side of his car, placing her back against it.

"Thank you," she said dryly. She appreciated the compliment, but Ka'ron was still on her mind.

"You okay today, baby?" he asked while placing kisses on her neck and face before kissing her lips.

"Yeah, I will be okay. I just have a lot on my mind that's all," she responded, placing her arms around his neck.

"Is it something you want to talk about?" he asked; his eyebrows rose wondering what was up. He prayed it had nothing to do with him.

Instead of going home where she should have gone, Mason talked her into coming back to his house with him. Autumn felt the cool sheets against her skin as she really thought about their relationship. She loved him but didn't feel like the relationship was making progress. He barely spent time with her, and of course, that was because, when he wasn't training, he was with other women more than he was with her.

"Mason?"

"Yes, baby," Mason responded as he pulled her closer to him.

"Have you ever thought about us just being friends?"

Mason sat up quick as hell with his face bunched in confusion. He didn't know where that question came from, but it didn't sit right with him.

"What do you mean, Autumn? Why the fuck you asking me that?"

Autumn glanced down and noticed that his fist was clenched, indicating that he was angry and most likely going to hit her. She sat up and slid to the edge of the bed just in case she needed to jump up.

"I'm just saying, maybe you need to be single. It's no point of us being together if you are going to cheat on me. I mean, you barely spend time with me anymore. At least once a week, some bitch is approaching me about you. I just feel if, it's meant to be, then we will find each other's heart when the time is right."

Mason sat in silence and calmed himself down. Everything Autumn said went in one ear and out the other. He didn't want to hear that, and he also wasn't letting her go. Although he knew she was right in a sense. He did want to have his cake and eat it too. He knew he wasn't ready for a real relationship, but he also didn't want her with anyone else.

"Is this about that nigga Ka'ron?" he asked through clenched teeth.

Autumn rolled her eyes while saying, "Oh my god. This has nothing to do with him. This is about you not knowing how to treat me, Mason."

Mason stood up and turned his back to her as he shut and opened his eyes repeatedly. All of a sudden, he punched the wall, causing her to jump.

"I am the only one for you. We not going to be friends, Autumn. You will continue to be my girl, or I will snatch that little flag girl position from you," he belted as he walked up on her getting into her face.

"Do you understand me?" He glared down into her eyes.

Autumn looked away from him, which made him snatch her face back up to look at him to see the seriousness in his eyes. She saw it and thought about all the things Hannah, her grandmother, and Ka'ron had been telling her. She wasn't going to be forced to be with anyone, especially this man who clearly had issues within himself. She wanted to help him, but obviously he didn't want it.

"Are you still taking those pills?" she asked as she snatched her face away from him only for him to grip her jaws harder and pull her face back up to look at him.

"None of your fucking business."

She studied his face for a minute before tears built up on the rim of her eyes before falling down her face.

"Get your hands off me, Mason. You don't want help, and you don't want me. Just leave me alone, and let me go. If you want, we can be friends, and I can help you through your issues. Then, we can revisit our relationship. Please."

Mason was already shaking his head as he let her go. He figured he knew what she needed. He hadn't fucked her in awhile. She noticed an almost demonic look overcome him as he reached and pushed his boxers down. His dick sprang out and caused her eyes to stretch wide in fear. She didn't want to have sex with him. She tried to jump to the other side of the bed, but he caught her foot dragging her back.

"No, Mason, no. I don't want to have sex with you like this. Stop," she screamed as she cried her heart out. She couldn't believe this was happening.

The comforter fell to the floor as he fought to rip her shorts and panties off of her body, which he successfully did. In his mind, she was playing hard to get, but she really didn't want to feel him in that way. He needed to man up and actually act as if he loved her and not treat her like some random hoe.

Mason pinned her legs to the bed as he positioned himself at her opening with her still struggling to get loose. However, she was no match for him. Her hands struck him a few times as she tried to get loose, and he smacked her and said, "Shut-up, you know you want this dick, girl."

He penetrated her, and she screamed in pain. He didn't make sure she was ready or anything. He just rammed right in her. She didn't want him, so her body wasn't ready for him. She continued to scream and cry as he pumped in and out of her. Sweat was dripping onto her face as he worked overtime to give her what he thought she wanted.

"Damn, Autumn. You are crying, but your body is saying differently." He didn't see anything wrong with what he was doing.

Autumn stared off in a daze as her body began to betray her. Her juices were flowing under her ass, making him think that she liked it, when really, she couldn't enjoy it because she didn't want it in the first place.

He bent down and tried to kiss her face, and when she wasn't receptive, he let go of her leg and grabbed her face with his thumb and first finger, forcing his tongue into her mouth.

"I can't believe you. I just can't!" she screamed as she slapped him.

She was definitely done now if she wasn't before. Mason growled as he shot loads into her. He collapsed on top of her as he caught his breath. When he could finally breathe, he got up and walked into the bathroom to wash himself off. He also retrieved another rag to wet it, and then he went into the room to wash her. He walked in to see her on her side crying. Her hair was all over the place, and the bed was fucked up. She was laying on the bare mattress. He tried to wipe her, but she snatched the rag and washed herself. She quickly grabbed her shirt and pulled it over her head. She didn't say anything to him.

"Baby, you good?"

Silence.

"Come on, babe; it was good. I know you feel better."

Silence.

"Well, it was good for me." He shrugged his shoulder as she watched him go inside his closet and reach for something. When she saw the pill bottle, she rolled her eyes. It wasn't her problem anymore.

He went and laid on the bed, pulling the comforter up over them and pulling her close like he didn't just rape her. Autumn continued to cry silently as she thought about how to get out of there.

"Goodnight, baby." He kissed her collarbone.

And again, he was met with silence.

******

It was two in the morning, and Autumn had yet to fall asleep. She had been crying silently off and on for hours. This man had beaten her, raped her, and cheated on her, and she was tired of it all. She had officially reached her breaking point. Raping her was the final straw for Autumn.

She grabbed her phone so that she could send a 911 text to Hannah. She texted Mason's address and told her to get there ASAP. She made sure her phone was on silent so that the notification wouldn't wake Mason up. Two minutes later, Hannah let her know that she was on the way.

Autumn slowly and carefully slid out of the bed, not wanting to take the chance of waking Mason up. She grabbed her tights, purse, and phone, and then she quietly walked into the living room where she got dressed. She held her breath as she tiptoed to the front door being sure not to make a sound as she slowly opened it. Once she was outside, she breathed a sigh of relief. She placed one hand on the door and the other on the doorknob as she pulled it closed. Mason's apartment was less than ten minutes away from Johnson C. Smith, so it didn't take long for Hannah to get there. When Autumn saw a gold, older model Toyota Camry, she rushed to the entrance of the apartment complex and slipped into the front seat where she broke down crying.

"What happened, babe?" Hannah rubbed her back to try and calm her down.

"Just go, Hannah. I will tell you when we get to the dorm." She continued to cry.

Hannah pulled off and headed to their school. She felt helpless. Her friend was hurting, and there wasn't anything she could do about it.

Chapter 20

The bright sun was peeking through the off-white blinds that were hanging in the window as Mason opened his eyes. He turned his body to the right to see how Autumn was doing. His eyes surveyed the room when he didn't see her body lying next to his. Her things were gone, and that's when he panicked.

Jumping out of the bed, his feet bolted across the carpet as fast as they could. By the time he was back in his bedroom, he realized that she was gone.

"Fuuuckkk!" he bellowed as his fists had a fight with the air.

He fell back onto the bed and grabbed his phone. He dialed her number and waited. He was on his sixth call and still didn't get an answer.

He didn't understand what the problem was. He didn't know why Autumn left nor why she wasn't taking his calls. It was like last night wasn't an issue for him. He thought he gave her what she needed, and that was the end of it. Now, he was beginning to think he went about things the wrong way.

He quickly got dressed, grabbed his keys, and was out the door. He practically ran to his car and hurriedly got inside. He checked the time as he was backing out of his parking space and realized he had to get there quickly before seven o'clock band practice.

As soon as he pulled up, he saw her and Hannah walking out the door, laughing. He swerved into a parking spot, causing a few students to jump back.

"What the fuck, nigga?"

"Watch where you going."

Some dudes were yelling at him, but he chose to ignore them. He had better things to do.

"Autumn, come here!" he screamed as soon as he jumped out the car.

Autumn ignored him and kept walking. He jogged to catch up with her, and his large hand gripped her arm and swung her around.

"Hold up now," Hannah said.

"Get the fuck off me!" Autumn screamed at the same time as Hannah.

"Why did you leave?" Mason seriously asked.

Autumn cocked her head to the side. "You really asking me that shit after you raped me?" she asked in a whisper, too embarrassed for people to hear her. Unfortunately, she wasn't speaking low enough.

Mason glanced around him and noticed that a few people stopped and turned after her accusation. His eyes landed back on Autumn, and that's when he noticed that she looked terrified. She was probably only standing there because people were around.

"How did I rape you? And don't be saying that shit out loud. Someone might believe you."

"And they should because it's true. I said no, Mason," she cried.

"You know what? I'm going to be late." She grabbed Hannah, and they stormed off.

"Don't walk away from me!" he belted.

When she continued walking, he ran up on her and grabbed her again. He pushed her hard, making her fall.

"Hold up now, potna; don't be hitting on a woman," some guy walked past and said. He was about to help Autumn up when Mason punched him in the face, causing them to start fighting. His friends broke it up as Hannah helped Autumn up. Autumn apologized to the guy as Mason tried to get out of the hold someone had on him. He was losing it. The guy who stepped in told Autumn to go ahead and leave while they had Mason.

"These niggas not going to be around forever, Autumn. You are mine; you can't leave me. I won't let you."

People were still standing around watching him make a fool of himself. People were whispering about him. No one had ever seen the track star act this way. Yes, he was a player, but that was something minor compared to him being off his rocker like he was now.

When Autumn was long gone, Mason was set free. He turned around, talking shit to everybody. After awhile, everyone dispersed. They no longer wanted to see him going on and on about how couldn't nobody touch him.

******

By the time band practice was over, the news of what happened between Mason and Autumn had spread like wildfire. On the way back to the dorms, a dozen people asked Autumn if she was okay. She held a subtle smile as she expressed that she was indeed okay. It was a lie, but she didn't want everyone in her business.

"If you want to jump him, we can," Hannah said as they neared their dorm.

Autumn burst out laughing, which was Hannah's end goal.

"Girl, you're crazy."

"I may be crazy, but I'm dead serious. He not going to keep messing with you; not my friend, nope," Hannah expressed as they entered their room.

"Thanks, Hannah, you always know how to get a girl out the dumps. What am I going to do though? Things are so messed up. Mason is not going to let me go so easily, and I have messed up things with Ka'ron." Autumn lowered her head into her hands as her shoulders shuddered. Hannah could tell she was crying. She stood from her bed to go over to her friend.

"Hey, hey, hey. Calm down; things will work itself out. If not, you have me."

"Stop it, Hannah. I'm serious."

"Me too, girl."

They just sat there until Autumn calmed herself down. She sighed and thought about her situation. She now understood that Mason wasn't for her. She questioned herself if she ever loved him or if he was just there for convenience.

She thought about her sister, Wynter, and her husband; that's the type of love she wanted. They seemed so perfect, and he treated her like a queen and their kids even better. She craved that and thought maybe that's why she was holding on. She then thought about her sister, Summer. Robert fucked up by cheating on her and having another baby, but she knew he loved her, and he treated her right. She didn't know what her sister was going to do about the situation, but she wouldn't be mad if she stayed because she felt their relationship was worth saving. Now Mason, he wasn't worth shit. He had too many issues that he wasn't willing to get help with. She understood that he wanted to make his parents proud, but overindulging in drugs wasn't the way to go. She had high hopes for them, but all of that was out the window, especially after he raped her and the way he acted out early. He made a fool of himself and her.

Autumn reached over to grab her phone after hearing her text alert go off.

Mason: I'm sorry.

She read the message and shook her head.

"That was his ass, wasn't it?" Hannah asked when she stepped out of the bathroom from her shower.

"Hell yeah," she answered as her phone chimed again.

Mason: You make me crazy, baby. I can't lose you.

Autumn's eyes rolled to the back of her head as she smacked her teeth, not believing a word he was saying.

"Let me get in this shower before we are late for class," Autumn said as she stood and headed to the bathroom.

******

Autumn could barely focus in her English class. It didn't help that Mason was sitting right beside her, attempting to get her attention. Everyone in the room could hear his whispers. Her body stayed facing forward as she tried to pay attention to her professor. Apparently, Professor Jackson heard him too and asked him to wait until after class for his outside conversation. Mason sunk down in his seat, feeling defeated because Autumn still wasn't paying him any attention.

When class was over, Autumn gathered her things and was headed out the door when Professor Jackson called for her to stay after for a minute. Autumn agreed but was trying to hurry out of there since fall break began tomorrow. She was going to go back to her dorm, pack, and head to either her sister's or grandma's house.

Autumn walked up to Professor Jackson with her lips curled at the ends as she asked what she wanted to talk about.

"Autumn, I noticed that you have not been yourself today. It seemed as if your mind was everywhere but the lesson. Now, I heard through the grapevine that you and your boyfriend got into it. Speaking from experience, I don't want a man to deter you from your dreams. You are a very intelligent, young woman, and you only need positive vibes in your life. You understand?" Professor Jackson gave Autumn a sharp look over her glasses as she glared down into her face.

"Yes, ma'am, I understand," Autumn replied.

"Good. I want you to know that my door and phone line are always open if you need me."

"I will keep that in mind; thank you Professor Jackson." Autumn reached to give her a half hug before leaving out of her classroom.

She was glad that Mason had to be on the track, or she knew he would have been waiting for her.

Chapter 21

"He did what, Danesha?" Ka'ron's eyebrows furrowed as his feet trudged across the floor.

"You heard me, boy. He made a spectacle of himself. It was terrible. And when he pushed her down—" Danesha was saying until Ka'ron cut her off.

"That nigga hit her again? You know what; I'm coming to get her." He stopped pacing the floor to put his shoes on.

"I saw her leave already. Fall break started after classes today."

"Damn. Now I feel bad for what we did." He let out an exaggerated sigh as his right hand dragged down his face.

"Well, fix it, bruh; you should know where she is. Go there and talk to her. From what you tell me and from what other people said today, that nigga is out of control. That dude is not for her, and she needs to realize it before it's too late."

Ka'ron's head was nodding up and down as he listened to Danesha. He was upset that she didn't call him, but knowing her, she was still in her feelings about seeing him with someone else. He knew one thing though; Mason was going to have to see him.

"And Ka'ron..."

"Yeah?"

"Someone mentioned rape."

Click!

******

Autumn was curled up in a ball in the bed. The covers were up to her neck, and there wasn't an inkling of light shining through the room. She had been in that same spot since she got to her grandma's house.

After what Ka'ron confided in her, Maggie was concerned about her granddaughter. She opened the door and flipped the light switch, causing Autumn to groan.

"Memaaaawwww, cut the light back off."

"Hell no, child. I've been in that living room waiting on you to come out all day and tell me what's going on with you. You come in here giving me a dry ass hello and then come straight to this room. You've been sulking enough; now tell me what's going on." Maggie snatched the covers off Autumn's body, and then placed her hands on her petite hips.

Autumn sat up and peered at her grandma with puffy eyes. Maggie wasn't the type of person to give up, so Autumn told her what was going on. She didn't leave anything out concerning Mason. Well, she left the rape out. She didn't know why, but she did.

"I knew I didn't like that nigga." Maggie sat on the edge of the bed.

"How long has this been going on, and why didn't you tell me or your sisters? Your sisters don't know, right?"

"No, they don't know. And I wanted to handle things myself. I thought I could help him with this steroid issue, but it backfired. He is still taking them too. He is abusing them by taking more than he should. Well, he shouldn't be taking them in the first place. He does it to please his parents. You should have seen the way his father belittled him for coming in second place." Autumn shook her head.

The more times she told this story, the more she realized how ridiculous it was for her to stay with him. She deserved better, and she knew that now. The only thing she was worried about was if he could really get her kicked off the team.

"The issues that Mason have with his father doesn't have anything to do with you, baby. Love doesn't hurt. Him hitting you shows he doesn't love you like he says. He may care, but obviously, it's not enough for him to treat you like you should be treated despite his issues with his father."

"I get what you're saying, Memaw, but he has also been threatening me saying if I leave him, he is going to get me kicked off the auxiliary team."

"I swear, the more you talk about him, the more I don't like him. How does he think he is going to get you kicked off the team?"

"I have no idea, but someone recorded an altercation I had with one of his side chicks…"

"Lord, he cheating too?"

"Just listen, Memaw, and yes, he always has according to others. But someone sent the video to the band director, and he told me if I get into anything else I will be suspended pending investigation of whatever incident."

"Mmm, mmm, mmm. I can't believe you let this go on so long. If something does happen, God got you, and the truth will come out. Don't worry about him," Memaw said as she reached to pull Autumn into a hug.

Autumn hugged her back and said, "Thanks, Memaw; you are the best." She kissed her cheek. Memaw stood up and said, "Now come on in here, and get you some neck bones, collards, and rice."

"Yeeesss, Memaw, you sure do know how to spoil a girl." They both laughed as they headed toward the kitchen.

******

Knock, knock, knock.

Autumn glanced over at Memaw who hunched her shoulders. Autumn stood to her feet and headed to the door. When she looked out the peephole, she smacked her teeth, opened the door, and then turned on her heels to go in her bedroom.

"Hey, baby; what you doing here?" She heard her grandma say.

Ka'ron followed Autumn with his eyes as he replied, "I came to see about her." He nodded toward Autumn with his head.

"I think she's mad at you. What I tell you," Maggie whispered as she punched him in the chest.

"Ooomph." Ka'ron pretended to be hurt as they both laughed.

"Go on back there, boy."

Ka'ron walked down the hall and grabbed the knob, but it wouldn't turn. He knocked gently with no answer. Autumn was on the other side of the door sitting on the bed in silence. She felt stupid and didn't know what to say to him.

"Autumn, open the door, baby girl," Ka'ron mumbled.

When there wasn't an answer, he knocked and asked her to open the door again. Seeing that he was getting frustrated, Maggie came down the hall and sad, "Step to the side. I got this," as she used a key to unlock the door. She walked away as Ka'ron opened the door and stood at the entrance, glaring at her through slits as she stared back at him wide-eyed.

"Why didn't you call me?" was Ka'ron's first question. He was serene on the outside, while on the inside he was furious. He waited patiently for her to answer, and when she did, she said, "Call you for what?"

She rolled her eyes to the back of her head, causing Ka'ron to chuckle as he closed the door and then stepped right in front of her.

"Don't give me that bullshit, Autumn. I'm hearing all this shit about you and your boy."

"And who told you that? Your little girlfriend?" Autumn mocked with jealousy dripping from her voice.

Chuckling again, Ka'ron shook his head as he said, "As a matter of fact yes, but she's not my girl. I was proving a point, which I succeeded. Ol' girl is my homeboy's sister. I was taking her to work as a favor because he couldn't. Now, cut the bullshit; what happened?"

Autumn was relieved that he wasn't talking to anyone else. Her hard exterior melted as she broke down.

"It was terrible, Ka'ron; it's like he got worse." Her shoulders heaved as she held her head in her hands.

Ka'ron gently grabbed her arm to pull her from the bed and circled his arms around her body. He kissed her neck as he comforted her. He wanted to know what happened but had to calm her down first.

Autumn's body molded perfectly into his, and she felt bad about the thoughts she was having. She didn't know how she was having impure thoughts at a time like this.

"You're okay now, Autumn." He pulled away after a few minutes and wiped her face. He grabbed a few Kleenex off the nightstand, held it to her nose, and said, "Blow."

She giggled and blew her nose at the same time.

"Ewwww," he expressed as he folded her snot in the Kleenex and held it to her nose again. After she blew, he grabbed another Kleenex and wiped the extra snot from around her nose before getting up to throw it away and wash his hands.

When he came back, he sat on the bed and pulled her onto his lap before asking, "Are you ready to talk now? I want to hear what happened from you."

Autumn laid her head on his shoulder and let it all out. She even told him how Mason raped her and acted like it was normal.

"The next day he came up to me as if he didn't do anything. He really thought I wanted him to do that. He has issues. I don't ever want to talk to him again."

Autumn could feel Ka'ron's breathing speed up. She lifted her head to look at him in time to see a tear fall.

Shocked was an understatement; she had never seen him cry before.

"I will kill that nigga," he seethed.

Autumn turned his head to her, shook her head, and said, "No, Ka'ron, you can't do that. Two wrongs don't make a right. Plus, I don't want you getting in trouble over me." She placed her forehead against his.

"But he hurt you, Autumn. If I wasn't playing games, you would have been with me. I was going to ask you to spend the night with me, but I wanted to see if you would get mad at me for talking to someone else. I'm sorry this happened to you, Autumn. I'm not playing, if that nigga even talks to you, I want to know," he said as Autumn wiped his face and then pecked his lips.

He pulled away and then dipped his eyes down her body. He was trying not to look at first, but she had on a pair of short ass spandex shorts with a tank top. Autumn's thighs were a beast, and he couldn't help but to give them a squeeze.

"This why his ass can't stay away right here. You got those thighs I want to lay on to stay warm. You got them thunder thighs." He paused for a minute and then asked, "But for real, are you okay? I mean, with him raping you. Do you need to talk to someone?"

"No, I am fine. I think if it wasn't him, I would be traumatized. Yes, he raped me because I was screaming no, but it's not like I haven't slept with him before, right?" she asked, but he could tell she was more or less asking herself.

Ka'ron thought that was the craziest thing he had heard. Rape was rape no matter if it was your boyfriend or a complete stranger. He frowned at her with his head cocked to the side but didn't say anything.

Autumn stood up and walked out the door to check on her grandma.

"You okay in here?"

"I'm fine, baby. Now, if Ka'Ron spends the night, I don't want to hear any moaning or screaming." Maggie smirked.

"What?" Autumn shrieked.

"Girl, bye, look at them little ass shorts." Maggie held a straight face.

"Now you know I had these on before he came."

"And you didn't cover up either. How long were you in that room by yourself?" Maggie asked with her head cocked to the side, waiting on Autumn's answer.

"You know what, Memaw? Goodnight." Autumn kissed her on the cheek and walked back into her bedroom. She passed Ka'ron and turned around to see what he was doing.

"Good night. I will see you in the morning. And don't worry, Memaw; there will be no screaming or moaning tonight." Ka'ron kissed Maggie's cheek before giving her a sneaky smile. He then turned around and dragged a laughing Autumn into the bedroom.

Chapter 22

Small lines of light could be seen through the room as the sun rose. The heaviness of the object on her side caused her to jump and sit up on the bed. When Autumn looked behind her and saw Ka'ron staring back at her instead of Mason, she was relieved. She sighed as she laid back down and pulled the cover over her head because she was embarrassed.

Ka'ron lifted the comforter over his head as well. Autumn's head was down toward her chest, causing him to lift her head with his finger. She had tears in her eyes as they bore into his. He pulled her close and draped his arm over her thick frame.

"What's wrong, baby girl?" Ka'ron spoke softly.

"I just..." She paused to wipe her eyes before she continued. "I thought I was at his house. I dreamed about him hurting me again. It was terrible. I don't think I'm okay," she spoke softly, almost inaudible.

"Listen, you don't have to front for me. I knew you weren't okay. Who would be after something so traumatizing? I'm here for you, you feel me?"

When she nodded her head, he pressed his succulent lips against hers and held them there a minute before parting her soft lips with his tongue. Their tongues intertwined, creating a dance that caused butterflies in her stomach. Her hand slid up the side of his body up to his head where it rested on the back of his thick neck.

"Mmm," Autumn moaned into his mouth as she pulled away.

She admired the perfect specimen in front of her. Who would have thought that an old family friend may be the one for her?

"I need you right now, Ka'ron. I need to erase him from my mind." She reached down grabbing his already hardened dick and said, "Looks like you want to give it to me."

Yes, Ka'ron wanted her, but they weren't there yet. He didn't want to bless her with sex until she was really ready. He shook his head from side to side and said, "Nah, you not ready yet."

He rolled her over onto her back and laid on top of her to kiss her down her body. His finger went into the waistband of her shorts and panties and then pulled them down her sexy ass long legs.

Her hand went down to her pussy as she dipped her fingers into her glistening canal. She pulled her shirt over her head and squeezed her left breast as she rolled her hips, trying to bring herself to an orgasm.

Ka'ron sat back on his heels as he licked his lips and watched her nectar drip out of her pink pussy. He smacked her hand away and took over by rubbing on her clitoris.

"Mmm," she moaned as he bent down and covered her pussy with his mouth, sucking her life away. He bit down on her clit, causing her to scream, and he had to cover her mouth. He didn't want to wake Maggie up.

"Damn, baby girl, you making it hard for me." He admired her before continuing to put in work. He latched onto her clit with his mouth as he entered her with his finger working it in a circle and then going as deep as he could before curving his finger like a hook, which caused her body to tremble as she came hard on his face. He continued to suck until she had no more to give.

Autumn's body continued to quiver as she came down from her high. Ka'ron's gaze dipped down her body as he watched her enjoy herself with her eyes closed. Her hair was spread all over her pillow, and she had a few pieces hanging in her face. She was beautiful to him. She deserved the best, and he was going to do his best to be that for her.

Ka'ron raised up and positioned himself to hover over her. He kept himself lifted with his right forearm as he removed the pieces of her hair that fell into her face.

"You will be mine; no need to rush. We need to set Mason straight, and you need to focus on your last year and a half of school. You are so special to me, Autumn.

It's driving me crazy that these things have happened to you. You try to be strong, which I know you are a strong ass woman, but like I said before, don't do that with me. I need you to be transparent, and I will be the same. You are the one for me. I knew it since we were younger, but out of respect for your sister, I never wanted to say anything until you were grown. Well, yo' ass grown now, and I think it's time for people to know. Your family already thinks they know, but they're not for sure. Well, Memaw knows, but she won't say anything." He dipped down to kiss her lips before rolling over to the side of her.

Autumn draped her leg across his body, and her hand went up to his face.

"Thank you." She leaned in for a kiss.

He kissed her back before responding with his own question, "For what?"

"Just for being who you are, for not judging me, and wanting the best for me," she concluded.

His hand traveled from her shoulder, stopping at her waist, and then slid to her voluptuous ass and said, "No need to thank me." He gave her ass a squeeze.

"You chillin' with me for fall break?"

"Now you know I have to be with my sisters too. I've been so busy with school and the band that I really haven't had time."

"You act like I can't be with you, woman, but no lovey-dovey shit in front of your sisters yet. They might kill my ass. How about we just let it flow? Whatever happens, happens. As long as Memaw knows, the rest will be okay," Ka'ron suggested.

"Okay, but I have a confession." Autumn smiled, which caused Ka'ron to glance at her with bewildered eyes wondering what she would say.

"I kind of already told Summer and Wynter I was feeling you. They were worried at first because of our age difference, but they will be okay with it."

"Man, you had me thinking we were hiding something." They both laughed.

Autumn kicked the covers off of them and rolled her naked body on top of him which made his dick rise again. When she felt it, she jumped up before he could even touch her body.

"I told you, you wasn't ready for this big thang here." He grabbed himself.

Bang, Bang, Bang.

"Get y'all nasty asses out that room and come eat." Maggie banged on the door and hollered.

Autumn shot a look at Ka'ron with wide eyes as they both burst into laughter.

"I don't know why y'all nasty asses laughing. Come on here."

"We coming, Memaw," Autumn yelled.

"You getting me in trouble, boy." She snickered.

He stood up as his eyes stayed fixated on hers and pulled his boxers down. Then he stood up straight, crossed his arms across his chest, and said, "Don't nothing about me say, boy. I'm all man over here, baby girl."

She stared at his dick while walking toward him licking her lips. She stood on her toes placing her arms around his neck. She kissed him while stroking his length until he was at his full-length.

"What you doing, Autumn? You going to get us caught, babe."

She didn't say anything as she kneeled down; she wanted to please him like he had pleased her. Her hands massaged the base of his dick as she sucked on the tip like a Tootsie Roll Pop. Spit dripped from her mouth down his shaft.

"Fuck," he whispered.

Her hands went to the back of his thighs as she devoured him. The tip of his dick reached her throat as she relaxed her throat muscles and let his pole hit her tonsils with no gag reflex.

"Mmm." The vibrations caused his toes to curl and leave an imprint into the carpet. He looked down at her perfectly sexy ass with low eyes watching her please him. She started to go hard making it wet how he liked it.

Before they knew it, he was cumming down her throat. He stepped out his boxers and collapsed on the bed with his arm laying across his face. His chest was heaving as he looked up at her standing in front of him and said, "You making this shit hard as fuck."

She straddled him and plopped her hot, juicy, wet pussy right on top of his hardened dick. She slowly ground against it while kissing his neck sloppily.

"Just give it to me, Ka'ron. I told you I need you."

"And you got me right here." He pointed to her heart.

"I know that but…" She tried her best to lift his thickness up and enter her, but he held on tight to her waist.

"Baby, we have all the time in the world for this."

She smacked his hands away, fighting with him until she was finally able to slide down on his long shaft. She held her breath until he was all the way inside her.

"Ohhh," she moaned. She felt she needed this. She wanted to erase the memory of what Mason did to her. She felt the way to do that was to fuck Ka'ron.

"Damn, fuck it. You want it? Then, act like you want this shit. Ride my dick, baby." He smacked her ass, causing her to sit up straight with a yelp and begin moving slowly in a circle. He matched her by moving his hips in a circle and tried to hit her spot. She switched it up on him and rhythmically bounced up and down on the ten inches of meat stuffed inside of her.

Bang!

"I done told y'all asses to come eat."

"We coming, Memaw. I'm waiting for him to get out the shower." She tried to sound as normal as possible, which was hard with his enormous piece of meat up her.

"Lying ass." They heard Memaw mumble as she walked away.

"We need to hurry," he said as he grabbed her waist and flipped her over. He pushed her legs all the way back so that her knees were touching the mattress. He watched himself go in and out of her, rocking her world. He didn't want to go to hard and have her screams be heard throughout the house.

"Yes, baby, mmmm." She pinched her nipples with her eyes closed.

"Open them fucking eyes while I'm in you; those sexy faces got me fucked up, baby." He dipped down to kiss her. He placed her legs over his shoulders as he drilled her with his lips still connected to hers.

"Is this pussy mine?" She heard his baritone voice as his lips brushed against his ear.

"Yes, baby. Only yours," she moaned exotically.

"What about Mason?"

"Who?" she moaned, causing him to smile.

Knowing they didn't have much time, he sat up and moved at a steady pace, grinding in her as he toyed with her clit. Her juices began to flow as she raised her ass off the bed to circle her hips.

"Show me what that pussy can do." He gave three powerful thrusts and caused her body to tremble as she came hard. When he felt himself about to climax, he pulled out and released on her stomach. He then collapsed on top of her, being careful not to smash her body. He kissed her collarbone a few times before gazing into her eyes and saying, "You are perfect, Autumn Irene Hart."

"So are you, Ka'ron Savion Davis."

After catching their breath, they showered and joined Maggie in the kitchen, who was giving them the side-eye.

Chapter 23

It had been two days since Autumn and Ka'ron had sex, and she had been on cloud nine ever since. They hadn't seen each other, but she promised to spend the weekend with him, and she couldn't wait.

She ended up having to block Mason's number; he was acting psychotic. She picked up the phone telling him not to call her anymore. As always, the conversation started off civil, and then he started going off on her. She didn't have time for his shit. She blocked that number with the quickness.

Autumn only had a year and a half of school left before graduation, and she didn't want Mason taking her down the wrong path. The only reason she felt as if she could work toward being with Ka'ron on that level was because she's known him all her life. If it wasn't for that, she would choose to not have another man in her life at all.

"Girl, what you over there smiling at?" Summer asked Autumn while passing her baby Robert.

"Nothing; can't a girl just be happy?" she responded as she blushed.

"Yeah, you can, but that's a different kind of happy. You finally gave Ka'ron a chance?" Summer questioned as she studied her sister's facial expressions.

"Me and Ka'ron are friends for now. He wants me to focus on school I already told you that," Autumn stated while blowing her cheeks out and crossing her eyes, making her nephew laugh.

"Yeah, you better be focused," Summer responded playfully.

She'd been with Summer all day since she hadn't let Robert back in the house yet.

"What's up with you and Robert, sis?" Autumn asked.

Summer sighed as she glanced down at the floor and then back up at Autumn before replying, "I really don't know. I mean, he did the ultimate. I love him, but can I really deal with him and his outside child? If I forgive him, I'm pretty much going to be in that child's life. Would I be stupid if I did?" Summer waited on her sister's answer.

"Honestly, I don't think you would be stupid. A blind man can see that man loves your ass to death. If you really love him, you wouldn't have any problems dealing with his child. You are a strong woman, Summer, and that's what it will take to take your man back. Look how hard he's been trying; there is no way that he would do that shit again. As far as Tracy, we can get in her ass if she jumps stupid," Autumn giggled.

Summer sniffed and wiped a tear that escaped from her eyes before she said, "Oh my god, you are so stupid, but thanks for making me feel better. I have been fighting with my decision since I had the baby. He was over here earlier, and I told him that I needed time to think."

"Now, just because I agree on you taking him back, I won't agree with you giving in easily," Autumn responded as she picked up her nephew's bottle and holding it up to his mouth for him to eat.

"Oh, believe me, I wasn't," Summer chuckled.

"Sis, you looking a little too comfortable handling him. Is there something you want to tell me?" Summer asked with a raised brow.

Autumn only laughed, causing Summer to ask, "A baby Ka'ron maybe?"

"Girl, bye. No babies until my career is off the ground. His ass better be patient with me though. I mean…" Autumn looked up at her sister with wide eyes after realizing that she had dropped the beans.

"Hell nah, no take backs, sis. I heard that. But for real, Ka'ron is a good man. I don't like your boyfriend. He has some shit with him."

Autumn's head shook from side to side as she removed the bottle from baby Robert's mouth, and then she lifted him up on her shoulder and gently patted his back so that he could burp. She looked toward her sister with tears threatening to fall and responded, "He isn't a factor anymore."

Summer was confused. Yes, she knew her sister wanted Ka'ron, but as far as she knew, she had a boyfriend that was holding her back.

"What's going on?" Summer caught a tear that fell from her sister's face.

"So much, Summer. Ka'ron had to rescue me a few times. He wants to kill him."

"For Ka'ron to convert back to his old ways, it must be serious. That nigga been putting his hands on you?"

Autumn nodded her head up and down, causing Summer to jump up and startle the baby and making him let out a loud cry.

"I'm sorry, baby boy." Summer sat back down. She was seething.

The two sisters sat and talked about everything that had been going on with Autumn. Summer expressed how upset she was that Autumn didn't come to her. Autumn understood that her sisters would always be there for her, but they were both going through their own things. Summer had her own relationship issues while Wynter had been having a few health issues that she'd been trying to hide herself.

Wynter happened to call and Summer filled her in on Mason. She too was upset and made Autumn promise not to keep anything like that from them again.

"If something would have happened to you, sis, we would have went crazy. Thank God you at least had Ka'ron," said Wynter.

"I promise I won't keep things from you again. Oh, and please don't tell Ka'ron I mentioned us. We were supposed to wait until this stuff with Mason blew over. We're sure he's not just going to let me go."

"That nigga don't have a choice if he wants to live," Wynter stated matter-of-factly.

"I know that shit's right," Summer expressed.

Autumn smiled while standing to place her nephew in his bassinet. She loved her sisters; they were all down to ride at any given time.

******

"I don't understand why her phone has been going to her voicemail since Tuesday," Mason said more so to himself as he pressed the red button to disconnect his phone.

"Damn, Mason; she probably got your ass blocked," Katrina sassed as she smacked her lips.

She was tired of his ass. She had been damn near naked in his bed for two days straight, and all he could think about was Autumn. Here Katrina was thinking that she was one-upping Autumn, when really there wasn't shit to gain.

"You think so?" he looked back at her.

"I'm telling you she did. Don't you have hangouts on your phone? Call her from that app. It will change your number," Katrina said as she crawled over to him and placed his flaccid dick in her mouth as he made the call.

When the phone began to ring, he heard that voice he loved so much, he knocked Katrina onto the floor. She was about to say something, but the look he gave made her shut her mouth.

"Hellooo." He heard Autumn say into the phone for the second time.

"Autumn, please don't hang up."

Click!

"Fuuuccckkk!" Mason bellowed.

Katrina smacked her lips as she stood from the floor.

"I don't understand why you chasing her, and she don't want to be chased. You got all of this in front of you, and you worried about a nappy-headed bitch," she said as her hands traced the curves of her body.

Katrina didn't really think Autumn was ugly, nor did she think her hair was nappy. She actually thought Autumn was beautiful, and her look was different. A lot of people claimed to be natural, but really her hair was beautiful and thick. Katrina was actually jealous.

"Why the fuck you keep running your mouth?" His large hands wrapped around her small neck. She clawed at his hands until he finally let go. She rubbed her neck as she wiped the tears from her eyes.

"Why would you—" she began to whisper before he yelled, "Shut the fuck up!"

He stroked himself until he was hard. He pushed her back on the bed and wedged himself between her legs.

"Mason, no; wait." Katrina tried to fight him off. She definitely was not in the mood to have sex with him. She heard Autumn say he raped her, but Katrina thought she was being dramatic. After all, how could your own boyfriend rape you, right? Well, now she believed it and wished she would have taken heed.

Chapter 24

"I swear I haven't been shopping in a long time. I need a job," Autumn said to her sisters as they pushed her niece and nephews through Northlake Mall.

"Girl, you are not getting nobody's job. If you need money, you know you can come to either one of us," Summer added.

"I know, sis. Oooo, let's go in Macy's. I heard they have hella sales." Autumn pushed Roman Junior's stroller toward the store.

Autumn was glad to be out with her family. She hadn't thought about Mason at all. She didn't know why he thought she would talk to him when he called from that unknown number. He really needed to get it through his head that she didn't want his ass. Her family knew the deal now, so it was on onsite.

"These shoes are everything." Autumn picked up a pair of casual Michael Kors sneakers.

"If you want them, go ahead and get them. They are forty percent off," Wynter stated as she reached in her purse and grabbed some fruit snacks to hand to her kids.

"Thanks, y'all." Autumn smiled as she grabbed a floor associate to grab her size from the back.

She sat down on the bench and removed her shoes off as she waited for the woman to return.

Wynter sat beside her and asked, "So has that no-good nigga tried to get in contact with you since y'all been on break?"

"Yes, I had to block him he was calling so much. Then, he had the audacity to call me from an unknown number. I hung up that phone so quick." Autumn laughed as the floor associate walked back over to them with a bright smile on her face.

"Okay, ma'am, here you go. I know you said you where an eight, but these shoes run small, so I also brought out an eight and a half." She took one of the shoes out the box, removed the tissue out of the shoe, and then handed it to Autumn to try on.

Once Autumn tried on the eight, she confirmed it was too tight and tried on the half size bigger. She was satisfied with that, so the associate, whose name was Tianna, took it to the register after Autumn thanked her.

"He is crazy; how you put up with him so long?" Summer inquired.

"Truthfully, sis, he didn't show his true colors until I fell in love, which now I'm questioning if it was love at all."

"It wasn't," Summer and Wynter answered at the same time.

They spent another thirty minutes in Macy's and two more hours in the mall before heading toward the exit.

"Autumn." They heard someone say, causing the three of them to stop in their tracks and turn around.

Autumn rolled her eyes, causing her sisters to become alert.

"What, Katrina? I'm not with the shits today."

"I'm not here to start trouble. I just wanted to apologize for coming at you sideways because of Mason. I know what you said was true because he did it to me yesterday." Katrina let a tear slip from her eye, causing Autumn to soften her stance a little.

"He raped you?" Wynter questioned.

Katrina responded by nodding her head up and down.

"Truthfully, Katrina, I'm sorry you had to deal with that. You know I know firsthand how that feels, but you brought it on yourself," Autumn let her know before walking off.

She didn't know what Katrina wanted, but she wasn't going to have sympathy for her. Call it what you want, but she didn't give a fuck.

******

Wynter dropped Autumn and Summer off at Summer's house before leaving. Autumn was going to stay with Summer tonight before going to Ka'ron's house for the weekend. She was excited to see how things would go between them.

"You hungry? I have some leftover meatloaf from yesterday," Summer asked.

"Yeah, I'll fix it."

"Oh, I know. I'm about to feed the baby," Summer laughed.

"Yeah, yeah." Autumn headed to the kitchen to fix her a plate.

The rest of the evening, they talked and played with baby Robert. At the end of the night, Autumn told her sister goodnight before going into the guestroom.

Ka'ron: Good night, beautiful.

She blushed as she read the text.

Good night. See you tomorrow, she replied to his text.

Ka'ron: Bet

She got up to take a shower, and once she was finished, she fell asleep with a smile on her face.

Chapter 25

You could see the glee written on Autumn's face as she packed a few outfits for her weekend at Ka'ron's. Summer and Wynter had helped her pick out lingerie when they were at the mall yesterday. She was skeptical about getting it, but she was talked into it by her sisters. They told her that she never knew what may happen. They didn't know that the two had already slept together; she wanted to keep that to herself.

"Girl, Ka'ron is not going to know what hit him when you put on that red shit; here." Summer walked into her closet and pulled out a pair of red, red bottoms and handed them to her sister.

"Oh my God. Thanks, sis," Autumn exclaimed as she hugged her.

"Just make sure you return them back the way you got them."

"I will." Autumn continued to pack.

Once she was packed and ready to go, she kissed her nephew and Robert's little girl before hugging her sister and letting her know that she would talk to her later. She placed her bag in the passenger seat before getting in and cranking the car. She sent Ka'ron a message and let him know that she was on the way.

When she pulled up, Ka'ron was waiting for her by the door. He walked outside to greet her. As he grabbed her bag, he smiled and snaked his free arm around her waist, causing her brown face to turn a deep reddish color.

"Hey, baby girl," he greeted as he pecked her lips.

"Hey, Ka'ron, come on; it's chilly out here." She wrapped her arms around herself as she began walking toward the front door.

He walked behind her and watched her hips sway with a smile. She could feel his eyes on her backside, so she put an extra twist to her hips.

"Aight, now, don't be doing that shit if you don't want me to drop this dick off in your pussy." He let her know while licking his lips.

"Boy stop." Autumn giggled.

"Baby girl, I done told you about that shit," he joked as he smacked her ass, making her yelp before he opened the door and let her walk in first.

Autumn always loved Ka'ron's house. He was a true bachelor, but his house had a female's touch to it. He swears he decorated himself though. His living room was decorated in red, gray, and a touch of black, just like his bedroom. His ranch style home was just enough space for him.

Ka'ron locked his door and led them to his room where he placed her bag in the chair in the corner.

"It smells good in here. You cooking?" Autumn questioned as she sat on the bed removing her shoes.

It was warm in his home, prompting her to remove her shirt to reveal a tank top. She had on tights, so when she stood to put her shoes in the corner, he could see all her goodies.

"Yeah, I'm cooking a little something for you. Go ahead and shower. I already took mine. By the time you get out, it will be time to eat."

Autumn walked over to him and stood on her toes to kiss him before going to do as he asked. She spent twenty minutes scrubbing herself clean. She was sure to use her Almond and Vanilla body wash from Bath and Body Works.

When she got out, she used the same fragrance to lotion her body before slipping on the lingerie set and pumps that her sisters helped her pick out. Her thick hair was wet and hanging around her face. She took a nervous breath before heading to the kitchen in search of Ka'ron.

His back was turned toward her as she entered the kitchen. She stood at the entrance with her right hand on her hip. He was pulling out two giant baked potatoes from the oven. They looked so good with melted cheese over the top. She saw sour cream, chives, bacon pieces, and mushrooms on the table in small dishes. She licked her lips ready to dig in. Her stomach growled loud as hell, prompting him to turn around wide-eyed.

"Daaammmnn, baby, when the last time…." He stopped mid-sentence and admired her perky breast. The red lingerie set fit her curves nicely. She had a leg garter pulled up her right thigh that he wanted to tear off with his teeth. His eyes traveled to her wide hips; he almost forgot that he had food in the oven.

"Damn, baby, let's hurry and feed you so I can have desert. How you going to come down here dressed with all that ass hanging out?" he asked as he shook his head while his eyes ran down her body again.

He placed the food in his hands down and grabbed Autumn by the waist. His hands slid down her waist tracing every last one of her curves as he bent a little to connect their lips. He kissed her passionately, letting her know that she was definitely turning him on.

He pulled away slowly and turned to pull out Autumn's chair before he pulled the steak out the oven and then grabbed two plates before putting a potato and a steak on each one. He placed the plates on the table and then grabbed the A1 steak sauce before walking to the refrigerator to get the pitcher of tea. After grabbing two glasses, he lifted the salad bowl and brought it all to the table. Ka'ron filled the salad bowls with salad and then slid one over to Autumn. He knew she liked balsamic vinaigrette dressing, so he was sure to toss the salad in it. After saying grace, they both dug into their salads. Silence filled the air until the salad was gone, and Autumn was finally able to taste the juicy steak.

"Oh my god, this shit is seasoned to perfection. Mmm."

"I can do a little something," he remarked as he loaded his potato up with all the sides placed on the table.

After dinner was finished, Autumn helped him clean the kitchen. She kept stealing glances at him. He had taken his shirt off when he went to the bathroom. She couldn't help but stare at his toned abs. He was just sexy for no reason.

"Come on; let's go chill in the living room." Ka'ron grabbed her hand pulling her in front of him as he hugged her from behind. His hands rubbed up and down her hips, making her shudder.

Ka'ron made her feel a different type of connection. He made it known that it was all about her. Unlike Mason, she knew for a fact that Ka'ron wouldn't hurt her. She felt it in her heart. She could really see this relationship going to the top.

He loved the smile that graced her face as he sat down on the couch and pulled her into his lap. He kissed her neck before saying, "I like seeing you this way."

"What way?" she inquired with her eyebrows bunched in confusion.

Ka'ron touched her lips gently with his finger as he replied, "Happy."

"It's because of you," she admitted as she stood up, reached for his hand, and said, "Let's chill in your room." She turned and led him into his bedroom.

Once inside, he removed his sweatpants before joining her in his king-sized bed.

"I've always had this fantasy," she blurted out as she lifted the remote off the nightstand and turned the TV on.

He turned toward her and wondered what kind of fantasy she had. She chuckled before saying, "Don't laugh at me, Ka'ron."

"Man, ain't nobody gone laugh at you," he said with a smile on his face.

"See, I'm not telling you; nope." She shook her head from side to side.

"Come on, babe." He began tickling her.

"Okay, okay, I'll tell you."   She giggled.

He stopped and propped his head on his hand waiting.

"I want to lay naked with you all night. I used to dream about it." She looked at him shyly.

He sat there saying nothing for a minute, and then he stood up to remove his boxers. He then got back on the bed and pulled her into a seated position to help remove the lingerie from her body. He gave her a look of approval as her perfect size C breasts sprang out toward him. He then prompted her to lift her bottom so that he could remove the bottom part from her skin. He laid back and pulled her with him.

"There," he said as he turned her head toward him to kiss her juicy lips.

Placing her leg over his, her warm pussy was on his thigh, causing his dick to come to life. He didn't want to make the first move though. He knew they had sex already, but she was emotional then. If she wanted to have sex, she would have to show him.

She browsed through Netflix and found a movie called *Deuce* with Larenz Tate that she'd been wanting to see. She pressed play and then snuggled close to Ka'ron. This is what she needed; his closeness to confirm how she really felt about him.

With Mason, it was just sex; good sex as a matter of fact, but there was no real passion behind it. Mason said the words but didn't show the motions. Mason couldn't cuddle without sex. Looking down at his hard dick, she knew Ka'ron was fighting with himself about what to do, and she appreciated that. He was putting her before his own needs. He respected her. He knew she was going through shit with that other nigga and was being patient. Her even agreeing to spend the weekend with him was enough for him. He couldn't say that after getting a taste of her pussy he didn't want it, because he did. However, he didn't have to worry because she was definitely feeling the same way, and before the night was over, she would be riding the fuck out of him.

"I bet that light skin nigga fake as fuck. He has been moving funny this whole time," Ka'ron blurted out.

"I think so too, but why ol' girl had to get killed. She ain't do shit," Autumn responded as she rubbed up and down his stomach.

"She must have seen something she wasn't supposed to. Probably whoever ol' boy was talking to in the car."

They both took turns stealing feels of each other until the movie was over.

"Oooooo. I told you." He laughed with his fist to his mouth.

Autumn laughed as she shut Netflix down. Ka'ron grabbed the remote and turned the TV onto the R&B music station and allowed it to play softly in the background. Once he placed the remote down on the nightstand, he laid back on the bed and closed his eyes.

"Fire We Make" by Alicia Keys featuring Maxwell could be heard throughout the spacious room. This used to be Autumn's song. It seemed as if the lyrics of the song touched her soul. She startled Ka'ron when she began kissing his chest, and then licked each of his abs that led down to his thick muscle between his legs. His dick jumped up and tapped her arm as if it was ready for her.

Her pussy was leaking, and she didn't want to waste any more time. She straddled him before engaging him in a passionate kiss. After the incident with Mason, she went to the doctor for an STD test and a pregnancy test. Both came out negative, so she was good for now. She knew that she would have to re-check the pregnancy test, but would deal with that later.

Autumn ground her hips against his swollen rod as they moaned into each other's mouths. Lifting her hips a little, she made room for him to grab himself and hold it at her opening. He rubbed his hardened penis along her slit, causing her to moan out in pleasure. He devoured her beauty as she slid down on his hardened shaft. He filled her to the hilt before placing his hands behind his head. He saw the fire in her eyes and the need to take control, so he would allow her for now.

She slowly moved her hips in a circular motion with her hand placed firmly on his chiseled chest as she gazed into his eyes. He glared back into her almond-shaped ones before his eyes fell onto where his dick met her pussy. He bit his lip and listened to her moans of pleasure.

"Damn, girl; shit." He smacked her plump ass, causing her to start bouncing on his dick after planting her feet flat on the bed.

"Fuuuck this shit wet." He watched as the juices from her pussy splashed between the two of them. He had the urge to pound her pussy and make her scream. It wasn't like they were at Maggie's, they could do what the fuck they wanted to. He lifted her up before standing and said, "Face down, ass up." He smacked her ass hard when she was taking too long.

When she was in the position of his choice, he climbed behind her and slid his glistening meat inside of her. His hand slid up the back of her head and gently pulled her hair, making her arch deeper. He held onto her hip as he began to give her deep strokes.

"Ahhh," Autumn screeched as she felt him deep inside her abdomen.

"Mmm shit." Ka'ron leaned down to kiss her sweaty back before he asked, "You love it, baby?"

"Yes, yes, yes," she continued to scream out in pain and pleasure as he showed her how a real nigga got down. He pulled out and flipped her over. This time, when he entered her, it was slow and sensual. Sweat covered their bodies as they spoke to each other with their movements. Ka'ron had Autumn screaming to the gods as he worked her body over. He left not an inch untouched. By the time he released his seeds, she had cum six times. Her body was so drained that she lay there while he prepared their shower.

"Come on, babe. I got you." He lifted her around his waist and walked into the bathroom. He stepped into the standalone shower and sat her on the shower bench as he washed himself a few times. Once he was finished, he stood her up and washed her body the best he could. He rinsed the both of them off one last time before lifting her and taking her into the room. After placing her in the chair in the corner, he replaced the bedsheets since they had wet spots all over them.

Ka'ron scooped a half-sleep Autumn up carrying her to the bed. He placed her down before handing her a bottle of water which she drank a few sips and then gave it back to him. He turned the music and TV off and got in bed behind her.

"You know I'm not ever letting you go right," he asked her while rubbing down her stomach.

"I hope not," she responded sleepily before fully falling into a deep slumber.

Chapter 26

Autumn was now back on campus. Ka'ron dropped her off this morning before he had to go to work. They stood outside by his car and showed each other affection before he helped her carry her bags to her room.

Katrina watched with hate as Autumn once again was with a fine ass nigga who seemed to care for her. She didn't know why she could never find a man to care for her that way. She watched how Ka'ron was gentle and loving toward her. It didn't help the way Autumn brushed her off at the mall. She now hated her more than ever. Even though Katrina didn't want to deal with Mason after what he did, she sat that to the side and picked up her phone to text to tell him Autumn was there being dropped off by some dude.

"I'll call you on my break, okay?" Ka'ron kissed Autumn once more.

"Okay, be safe," she responded.

Ka'ron opened the door to come face to face with Mason. Mason gawked at him with clenched fist. You could hear his teeth; he was grinding them that hard. Ka'ron glanced back at Autumn, who seemed terrified.

He turned around for a minute, not even caring about turning his back to Mason. He held each side of Autumn's face and said, "Look at me, baby girl."

Once her eyes left Mason to him, he said, "You never have to be afraid of anything while you're with me. I will protect you from whatever threats come your way, even if that means I have to pull the tool out. Understand?"

She nodded her head up and down as she placed her hands on top of his, causing him to peck her lips.

"What the fuck? You kissing on my girl?" Mason bellowed as he damn near ran toward Ka'ron.

Ka'ron was unfazed as he quickly turned around blocking his punch and catching him in the jaw. The punch was so hard that Mason stumbled and fell to his knees.

"Nigga, don't you ever run up on me," Ka'ron spoke with a calmness that made Mason quiver. He grabbed his neck and made him turn toward Autumn as he pointed to her and said, "You see that queen right there? That's me, you little bitch." He let Mason go and kicked him hard in his right leg.

"If you fuck with her again, I will break your fucking legs, and you won't be able to run, nigga. Fuck with me if you want to. Now, get the fuck out," Ka'ron spat as he turned to Autumn, who was covering her mouth and was wide-eyed. She relaxed as Ka'ron touched her shoulder and said, "I got you; you're with a real nigga now."

This time he pulled her close, moving his hands to her ass and tonguing her down as his eyes stayed fixated on Mason as he slowly stood up.

Autumn noticed the people who gathered by the door and Katrina stood out. She was smirking lustfully at Ka'ron like she was turned on. In fact, she was. Her panties were wet as she watched Ka'ron check Mason. Autumn caught her lick her lips, prompting her to pull back from Ka'ron and walk to the door just as Mason ran out.

"Bitch, why the fuck you lusting over my man? You may have fucked Mason, but he will never fuck you," she spat while pointing at Ka'ron.

"Bitch, bye, if that nigga get a taste of me, he will never come back to you. What's up, baby?" Katrina boldly asked Ka'ron.

At that point, Hannah walked through the hall and wondered why everyone was surrounding her door. When she got close, she saw Autumn lunge toward Katrina, but Ka'ron held her back.

"Nah, baby, this ugly ass fake bitch ain't got shit on you. Worry about your education, and I got the light work." He turned toward Katrina and said, "Keep fucking with my girl, and I will have somebody break your fucking arms. How are you going to twirl a flag when your shoulders are dislocated? This goes for everybody; stop fucking with my girl." He turned to

Hannah and said, "This goes for her too. So spread the word."

Ka'ron wasn't with the shits. If Autumn had beef, so did he. People she cared about, he cared for too. That's why he included Hannah because that was Autumn's best friend.

"Fuck y'all." Katrina stormed off with everyone laughing at her.

After that, everyone began to disperse. The three of them went into the room and Hannah asked, "What the hell happened? I saw Mason run out the building like he was running from the devil."

"Ka'ron had to knock his ass out. I don't think he will be a problem anymore though. Him nor Katrina."

"Good. I knew you were going to get with bae," Hannah said, causing Ka'ron to laugh.

"Oh, so she been wanting a nigga?"

"Uhh huh." Hannah smiled.

"Hannah, you supposed to be my friend."

"I am, bitch; that's why I'm glad you with the right nigga." They all laughed.

"Aight, babe, I have to get to work. If anything, call me." He kissed her once more before leaving.

Chapter 27

It had been a month since the incident with Ka'ron and Mason. For the first week, Mason would look at her with a menacing glare whenever he saw her. Now, it was occasional. He still claimed he loved her to anyone who would listen, including his parents.

His mother and father told him to leave it alone. That if it was meant to be, then it would be. Of course, Mason omitted parts of the story, not wanting his parents to know what he really did.

Ka'ron would come on campus often to see Autumn or to pick her up. Every time Mason saw them together he would get upset. His pill popping had gotten out of control. He had doubled up on most days, causing him not to think with a clear head at times.

Autumn and Ka'ron were still hanging in there. They didn't really have a title yet, but Ka'ron often reminded her that since she gave him the pussy, she was his. She had no problems with that.

"I'm ready to get this over with so I can go eat this good ol' food my grandma cooked," said Autumn to

Hannah as they stood on Stonewall Street waiting for the Thanksgiving Day Parade to begin.

"Girl, who you telling? I know my momma cooked a feast," Hannah responded.

At the sound of Katrina's voice, everyone began to get in formation. The auxiliary squad was positioned in the front while the dance team was behind the band.

By the time everyone was ready, the drumline kicked off the cadence, instructing the band to begin marching.

Autumn took in the cheers as they did their thing. This was what Autumn lived for. She loved being on the squad, especially when it was time to perform.

By the time the band marched all the way to North Tryon Street, everyone was exhausted.

"Good job, guys," Sammy, the drum major, praised the band for a job well done.

Autumn's family was waiting for her at the finish. The band was allowed to leave with their family members who came after their instruments were packed on the bus.

Autumn caught up with her sisters, grandma, and Ka'ron, and then headed to Maggie's house.

The first thing Autumn did was get in the shower. As she was washing, she felt a whiff of cool air. Peeking out the shower curtain, she saw Ka'ron's pearly white teeth before he bit his lip.

"Oh my god, what are you doing in here?" Autumn asked in surprise since her family was in the house.

Ka'ron locked the door and then pulled his shirt over his head before unbuckling his jeans and letting them fall to the floor.

"I want some of my pussy," he whispered.

"Are you crazy?" she responded, knowing it would be hard for her to stay quiet with him inside her.

As he stepped in the shower, she couldn't help but lick her lips at his well-defined body. Ka'ron stayed in the gym, and you could definitely tell.

"It will be quick, I promise." His lips crashed into hers, not being able to wait another minute.

She had no come back because, as soon as he touched her, her body melted against his. Ka'ron's hand traveled down her stomach and caressed her pussy. She moaned as she opened her legs wider for better access. He felt that she was ready for him which caused him to lift her in the air and slide his hardness inside of her.

He turned so that her back was against the shower wall, and then he placed both her legs over his arms before sliding in and out of her with long, deep strokes. His face went to her exposed neck as he gently sucked and sent her over the edge.

His strokes were strategic, and he knew exactly where to hit to make her cum. He focused on that spot that caused a moan to slip out her mouth. She put her face against his shoulder to drown out her moans. After Ka'ron hit that spot once more, her body trembled as she came, causing him to pull out and cum as well. He caught his breath before slowly letting a shaky Autumn down. Her arms went around his neck as she initiated a passionate kiss.

"Girl, you got me trippin'. Got me wanting this pussy at all times." He bent down to grab her rag out the tub and washed her before grabbing another rag and washing himself. They got out, got dressed, and left the bathroom one at a time to join the others.

Summer was giving the two the side-eye as Autumn tried her best to avoid her sister's gaze, while Ka'Ron only laughed.

Thanksgiving was in full swing. The food was good, and the time with family and friends was even better. After picking a secret Santa, the family sat in the living room for another hour before everyone packed up some food and went to their homes. Autumn left with Ka'ron since she didn't have class until Monday.

******

"You want to hit the movies?" Ka'ron asked as he pulled out onto the street. He placed his hand on her thigh as he waited for her answer.

"Ooooo. Yes, I've been wanting to see *Jigsaw*."

"Oh hell naw, I'm not with that scary shit," Ka'ron said matter-of-factly, causing Autumn to laugh.

"Ahhh the big baby is scared," she mocked as she rubbed the back of his neck.

"I'm not saying all that; I'm just saying."

"Sounds like you scared to me. Don't worry. I got you."

Needless to say, they ended up at Northlake AMC watching *Jigsaw*. Autumn laughed the whole time as she watched Ka'ron flinch. The movie was scary though. The both of them stayed hugged up and tripped off how stupid the characters were. Who goes toward the danger?

It was close to midnight when they got to Ka'ron's house. After a nice, warm shower, they were both in bed naked with their bodies intertwined.

"Did you ever think we would be here?" Autumn stared at him through the darkness, watching his lips pull into a smile.

"Yes. I knew that we would get here, just didn't think it would be so soon," he admitted.

He knew that he would eventually get his woman. At first, he was going to let her finish school before he pursued her, but when Mason started fucking up, he decided to ease on in there. It was a good thing that Autumn was feeling him anyway.

"You just knew you were going to get me, huh?"

"I always get what I want, baby girl," he said as he rolled over on top of her and pecked her lips a few times before poking at her entrance. He entered her slowly, and they made love until they fell asleep.

Chapter 28

The next morning, Autumn woke up bright and early to take a shower. She wanted to surprise Ka'ron by cooking him breakfast. She was just taking the last French Toast out the pan when he walked into the kitchen and hugged her from behind.

His smell invaded her nostrils, causing her to bite her bottom lip as memories from their lovemaking last night crossed her mind.

"Mmm," she moaned as he kissed her neck and then stepped away, stealing a piece of bacon.

"This looks so good, baby," he praised as he glanced over the spread of food: French Toast, eggs, bacon, and cheese grits. It was perfect for the way his stomach felt at the moment.

"Thanks, baby." She poked her lips out for a kiss.

After his lips touched hers, she asked, "Can you get us something to drink and then sit down while I fix our plates?"

He did as she asked while Autumn grabbed two saucer plates and placed two French Toast each on them before placing them on the table. She then grabbed two regular plates and loaded them with cheese grits, eggs, and bacon and then placed them on the table. She grabbed the grape jelly and syrup and then joined Ka'ron at the table.

After adding a teaspoon full of jelly to their grits, they said grace and then dug in.

"This is so good, baby," he said, causing her to smirk.

"Well, they say the key to a man's heart is through his stomach."

"Nah, baby girl. The key is that tight wet pussy you got." He smirked.

"What? Shut up, Ka'ron." She giggled.

After finishing their food and cleaning the kitchen. They decided to go catch some of the Black Friday sales at the mall.

******

Autumn and Ka'ron walked through the mall hand-in-hand. Ka'ron had a few bags in his hand filled with Christmas gifts for his family along with Autumn's.

"Look at these punk bitches." They heard someone say from behind them.

Ka'ron stopped in his tracks and turned around to see Mason along with four other niggas. He dropped

Autumn's hand and their bags. He walked up in Mason's face with Autumn trying to hold him back.

"Babe, he's not worth it; come on." She pulled on his arm, but he shook her hand away and gave her a look that made her back away.

Mason's friends surrounded Ka'ron as if they were going to jump him. Ka'ron gawked at each of them with a menacing glare.

"Nigga, you got something to say?" Ka'ron inquired not even affected by the fact that these other niggas were surrounding him.

"Don't think you bad, nigga. I will whip your ass." Mason tried to act bad in front of his friends.

Ka'ron chuckled as he looked around him and said, "What? Y'all going to jump me? We both know I already whipped your ass, so what's up?"

The guys closed in on Ka'ron with clenched fists.

"You want me to knock his ass out, bruh?" one of the guys asked Ka'ron.

Ka'ron laughed loudly as he pulled a gun from his waistband, causing Autumn to gasp.

"Ka'ron, no; security is coming."

Ka'ron didn't care. He was licensed to carry a gun on him, and this particular gun was registered, so he didn't care one way or another.

With their eyebrows raised and lips formed in an 'O', the guys stepped back behind Mason who stood wide-eyed, staring at the gun.

"Yeah, niggas. It's real over here. I got something for you though, my nigga," Ka'ron belted as he slid his gun back in his waist before turning to Autumn, who was trembling. He touched her face and kissed her a few times.

"It's okay, babe."

She nodded her head up and down. She trusted Ka'ron with her life, and the shit he just did had her scared and turned on at the same time.

"Is there a problem here?" security walked up and asked.

Ka'ron looked up and tried to figure out why Mason and his friends were still standing there.

"I don't know, is it?" Ka'ron glanced at Mason.

"No, no, no. We straight." He and his friends then scurried away.

"I guess not," Ka'ron said to security.

Security nodded and then walked away. Ka'ron picked their bags up, grabbed Autumn's hand, and continued through the mall.

"I don't think he's ever going to get it," said Autumn sadly.

"Oh, he will, and very soon." Ka'ron smiled deviously.

Autumn didn't know what he was up to, but she trusted that he was going to take care of it.

Chapter 29

Class had just ended, and Autumn was headed to the library to start her research on a paper she had to write about child education. For some reason, Autumn loved to write papers; it was her thing. She always aced them with flying colors.

She found a table for her and Hannah since she knew that she would be right behind her after her computer programming class was over. She sat down and removed her notebook from her bag. She then got up to find a few books that would help her with her paper.

As she was browsing the aisle of child education books, someone cleared their throat. It was Jalisa, Katrina's friend, who was on the auxiliary squad with her.

"You need something?" Autumn asked.

Jalisa fidgeted for a minute. Autumn could tell that she was nervous about something.

"Umm, I need to talk to you about Mason."

"I don't care about him. If you want to fuck him, go ahead."

"No, Autumn it's not that. It's just that I heard you say he raped you. At first, no one believed you," she whispered, not wanting anyone to overhear their conversation.

"Okay and…"

"Well, you're not the only one. He raped me too after the Kappa party last week. I didn't tell anyone because I was embarrassed. Katrina didn't know until yesterday when the team had practice, and you didn't have to come. Apparently, some of the girls he slept with didn't give consent. On top of that, he takes some type of pills."

Autumn gazed into Jalisa's watery eyes and saw nothing but the truth.

"Steroids."

"Huh?" asked Jalisa.

"He is taking steroids; a lot of them. I tried to get him to stop. He experiences 'roid rage according to my boyfriend. It's dangerous. So what do you want from me?"

"Well, we decided that he can't get away with this. We want to take action and were hoping that you would join in," Jalisa pleaded with worried eyes.

Autumn thought for a minute. Mason definitely needed to pay. She would have to know what was going to happen.

"When y'all get the details, let me know. I wanted to erase him from my life, but I do want him to pay."

Jalisa agreed to get back to her and they went their separate ways. Autumn found the books she needed and found Hannah at the table when she went back.

"Girl, how you know where I was sitting?"

"Nobody has that Afrocentric ass bookbag but your ass." Hannah pointed toward Autumn's bookbag and laughed.

"Ha, ha, ha, bitch. But Mason has been busy. Jalisa just had a convo with me."

"Please don't tell me he raped her too." Hannah looked around to be sure no one was in earshot.

"Apparently her and others. They tryna do something about it. I told her to let me know the plan. I'm just not so sure I want to be involved."

"Autumn, he definitely should pay. I'm not going to tell you what to do because it's ultimately up to you. Either way, I'm here for you," Hannah expressed as she got up and hugged Autumn before sitting down so they both could get some work done.

******

Later that night, Mason sat on his couch with a bottle of Hennessy, a blunt, and Hydrocodones he purchased from some white dude on campus. He no longer indulged only in the steroids. He wanted to feel high, which is why he turned to Hydros.

His head felt light, the whites of his eyes were red, and his eyes were lowered to slits. He looked over at the girl who he met last week and smacked her bare ass cheeks. Mason was out of control, and no one could save him but himself.

"Come take care of this," he slurred while pointing at his hardened dick.

She had been cooperative since she got there, so he didn't have to force her to do anything. She stood and lowered down on her knees and took him fully into her mouth after lubricating his dick with her saliva. The heightened feeling from the drugs and her wet mouth sucking him nastily had him feeling like he was in heaven.

"Ahhh fuck, Autumn." His head fell back on the couch.

He slowly felt the pressure let up, which caused his eyes to pop open and his head shot up. He glanced down at the girl, whose name he couldn't remember, and asked, "Fuck you stop for?"

"You just called me another bitch name," she answered.

He sat quiet for a second and realized that he did, but in no way would he admit it.

"Girl, I didn't call you shit. Finish sucking my dick, bitch."

"Ahhh, hell naw." She attempted to stand up, but he grabbed her hair and yanked her back down.

"I said finish, bitch."

She became alarmed that she was in danger. She pretended as if she was going to finish, and as he put his head back, she bit his dick and then punched him in in his balls as hard as she could. He doubled over in pain. She jumped up and grabbed her pants, shirt, and purse on the way to the door. She noticed him trying to get up and bolted out the door naked and all. She didn't get dressed until she was in the car with the doors locked. When she noticed him easing his way down the steps, she said fuck it, cranked her car up, and drove home half-naked.

Mason went back in the house when he saw her pull off. He went and laid across his bed, grabbing his phone trying to call Autumn. Of course, she didn't pick up which made him angry.

He thought about heading to her dorm, but he knew he wouldn't be able to get in since the doors locked from the inside at 9 p.m. A low growl escaped his lips when he thought about how out of control his life was right now. It was all because he couldn't stay faithful to the woman he claimed he loved. He also wondered why he let his parents get to him to the point that he would start abusing steroids. He knew he had an addiction when he wouldn't stop like Autumn asked him to. He regretted not listening to her; now he had a greater addiction.

He was telling himself just to leave the situation alone, but his mind and heart was telling him to fuck Ka'ron and get his girl back.

Chapter 30

The week before Christmas break came quick. There was one home game left before football season was over. Although this wasn't the last time the band would meet because they still had competition until February. It would be the last time this year that they performed on the home field for the football team and their fellow Golden Bulls.

The whole band was on the field for their last practice before Saturday. The cold air hit Autumn in the face, and her hands were cold as ice, but she would never show that she was freezing; just like the rest of the band, they were dedicated.

The drumline hit the cadence right before their solo as everyone else stood motionless and waited for them to finish. Practice went by perfectly. The band screamed and clapped once they were given the "at ease" command by Sammy, the drum major.

"Alright, ladies, great job today." Katrina clapped her hands before walking off.

Jalisa walked up to Autumn and asked, "Have you made a decision?" She looked around to be sure Katrina wasn't looking. She wasn't scared of her or anything, but when she finally said something to Katrina, she said she didn't want any parts.

"I'm still not sure, but I'm leaning toward helping out. I'll get back to you in a few days," Autumn said, and Jalisa nodded her head and walked off.

Autumn waited for Hannah to walk up to her before they made their way to the band room to put away their flags.

"You trying to go out tonight?"

"Nah, I'm going to see my nephew once I shower and get dressed. I'll probably be there for awhile."

"Oooo, can I go?" Hannah asked.

"Yeah, you can come. My sister would be happy to see you," Autumn said as she placed her flag where it belonged.

The two walked out of the band room and headed toward their dorm.

"Autumn, let me holla at you."

Autumn heard Mason's annoying ass say. Her eyes fixated on Hannah, and she kept walking. She had nothing to say to this fool. He looked unkempt. His face looked like a wooly mammoth, and his hair looked as if it hadn't been cut in over a month. His clothes were wrinkled and didn't match like he didn't care. She had heard around campus that he was falling off, but she didn't pay it any mind. Also, his performance on the track hadn't even been as good as it once was. He was still winning, but his time goes up a couple seconds each week. Even with all that, she had no sympathy for his ass.

He continued to call her name, getting angrier at the fact that she wasn't responding. When they were close to their dorm, she sighed in relief when she saw Ka'ron. He was leaning against his car when he saw Mason, immediately causing him to perk up.

"Aye, nigga, what I tell you?" He stood up and headed their way.

Mason stopped in his tracks wide-eyed as his neck turned in all directions for an escape. As Ka'ron got closer, he turned around and took off running.

Autumn and Hannah fell out laughing along with a few others that were standing around while Ka'ron shook his head standing there. There was no way that he was going to waste his breath chasing that fool.

"Damn shame, he can hit a woman but running from a nigga." Someone was heard saying as they too laughed.

Ka'ron stepped to Autumn and pulled her close. She wrapped her arms around his neck, and they engaged in a passionate kiss.

"Mmm," escaped from Autumn's lips.

"Ewwa, get a room. I'm going to take my shower," Hannah joked as she walked off.

"You okay, baby? Did he touch you?" Ka'ron asked once they pulled back.

"No, he followed me from the band room, and I didn't say anything to him. I'm so glad you were here," she expressed as she kissed his lips once more.

"We were about to go see my nephew; you want to come?"

"Nah, I have a few errands to run. I just needed to lay eyes on you for a minute, baby girl." He palmed her ass while kissing her neck.

She loved the public displays of affection that he always showed. He wasn't afraid to show her how much he loved her. She felt the best decision she made was letting him in and letting that dead weight of a boy, Mason, go.

"Okay, babe. But look, Mason is in more trouble than we thought. He raped more women on this campus than we knew about. They all got together and are in the process of a lawsuit. One of the girls came to me and asked if I wanted to be a part of it. What do you think I should do?" Autumn asked as they walked back to his car hand-in-hand.

"I think that whatever you decide, I'm behind you. I wanted to knock that nigga out for fucking with you. But if you want to go this route, it's cool. When all of you come together, his life will be over anyway. I still might break that nigga legs though," he stated seriously.

Autumn positioned her body between his legs.

"I swear that's how I know you're the man for me. Plus, I couldn't take it if you got locked up for killing him or something." She laid her head on his chest, and Ka'ron cupped the back of her neck with his right hand before he bent down a little to kiss her forehead.

"Please, a real nigga don't get caught." He chuckled.

"Let me go, though. Give me a call later."

Autumn stood on her toes to peck his lips a few times before saying their goodbyes.

******

"Man, Mason, you are really trippin'," Quan, Mason's teammate and friend, said to him as they sat in Quan's dorm room. He was one of the people who was with Mason when they saw Ka'ron in the mall. He was down for it then, because he wasn't going to let his boy get his ass beat, but now he felt things were getting out of hand.

When Mason ran off, he ran straight to Quan's room. He wasn't fooling with Ka'ron, not straight up. He knew Ka'ron's threat was real, and he didn't want his legs broken. He saw the look in Ka'ron's eyes when he threatened him and knew that he would make good on his promise. He may be out of it, but he knew he needed his legs to be able to run.

"What you mean, man?" Mason asked confusingly.

It was sad how Mason didn't think he had done anything wrong. He felt that Autumn belonged to him. He also felt that if a woman came to his apartment or invited him over to their house, then they wanted the 'D'. Even if they said no, they still wanted it, or they wouldn't be in his presence. He had an ignorant way of thinking.

"Man, you my homey, so I'm gonna keep it real wit'cha bro. You falling off. You look rough as hell. I've never seen you look like a bum. And it's all because of ol' girl. Is she really worth it?" Quan inquired as he sat down across from Mason.

Mason's jaw was tight. He was grinding his teeth so hard you would think his teeth were cracking.

"She is, Quan. I love her."

"Apparently you fucked that up though, bro. You love her, but I'm hearing words being thrown around like abuse and rape. What's up with that, Mason?"

"It's all a misunderstanding." Mason fidgeted with his hands.

He knew damn well it was not a misunderstanding.

"Then, I hear you going around raping other women on campus. Is it true?" Quan asked.

"Man, them bitches wanted it just like I did. What's up with all the questions though, Quan?"

Quan was silent for a minute. He realized that the rumors were true. His homeboy was an abuser and a rapist. Who would have thought?

"Bro, you got to get the fuck up out of here. You abusing women, raping women, and you're on drugs. I can see that shit. You are falling off, bruh bruh. If you don't get help, forget about Autumn, you got to go. What's it gon' be?" Quan stood walking toward his dorm room door.

Mason was seething. He didn't have time for this shit. He stood from his seat and walked toward the door while he said, "Fuck you, nigga. I don't need help. When I take my girl back, I'll be straight."

He walked out the door as Quan shook his head thinking, *He is a lost cause.*

Chapter 31

Autumn and Hannah exited the car and walked to Summer's front door. After pressing the doorbell, Summer answered the door and hurriedly walked away before the cold hit Lil' Robert.

"Hey, sis."

"Hey, Summer."

Autumn and Hannah greeted Summer simultaneously.

"Hey, y'all," she responded, giving them both a hug.

Summer handed the baby over to Autumn so that she could finish fixing him a bottle of milk. Autumn and Hannah sat on the couch and played with the baby.

"He is so adorable." Hannah smiled as she stuck her finger out so that Lil' Robert could grab ahold to it, which he did.

"Thank you," Summer responded when she walked out of the kitchen and handed Autumn a bottle. "Here, it's time for his chubby cheeks to eat. How was practice?"

"It was lit, sis. The band director has the band playing "Talkin' Out the Side of Your Neck" in the stands. Our dances are even better."

"Okay now, I can't wait to see it."

Autumn continued to feed her nephew, stopping to burp him when he began to spit milk back out.

"Where is LaTrina?" Autumn asked.

She was referring to Summer's boyfriend's other child. He cheated on her to create a beautiful life. Apparently, the woman he cheated with wasn't worth two cents. She up and left the baby and hadn't looked back. It was said that she was with her ex, and he didn't want an outside baby.

"She is upstairs sleeping. That little girl is such an angel. I love her already. I can't believe her mother, if you can even call her that," Summer said as she thought about Tracy, LaTrina's mother.

"Wait, who is LaTrina?" asked Hannah.

"That's right, so much has been going on I haven't talked to you." Autumn turned to Hannah wide-eyed.

After getting permission from Summer, Autumn ran down the situation with her sister.

"Damn, some people don't need to get pregnant. Well, I commend you, Summer; not many women would take in their boyfriend's baby."

"Hey, it's not the baby's fault. She is so sweet and deserves parents who will love her." Summer smiled.

Hannah loved Summer. She had such a good spirit about her. She thought Summer was the sweetest.

Keys jiggling in the door caused the three women to turn their necks toward the door. A second later, Robert walked through the door, and Summer stood up to make her way to her man.

"Hey, baby," she greeted him with a hug and kiss.

"What's up, baby. Hey, Autumn and Hannah," he responded after pulling away from Summer.

"Hey, bro."

"Hello."

Autumn and Hannah spoke to Robert.

"Where lil' momma?" Robert asked after bending down to kiss his son.

"She's in their room asleep," Summer responded.

"That's what's up. I'm going to fix me something to eat. I'm starving. Ka'ron had me on the courts today."

Autumn perked up and blushed at the mention of Ka'ron's name. Summer looked over at her sister and smiled. She hadn't seen her blush over anyone like this.

"Nah, baby, go freshen up. I will fix you a few sandwiches to hold you over until I cook."

"You're the best, baby." Robert kissed Summer once more before disappearing up the steps.

"Relationship goals," Hannah belted as she danced in her seat, causing Summer and Autumn to laugh.

"I know right. I hope me and Ka'ron get to this point. You guys' love shows," Autumn said as she looked down at her sleeping nephew.

"If it's meant to be, you will. I love Ka'ron like a brother. I think he is good for you," Summer admitted as she grabbed Lil' Robert from her sister's arms.

"I'll be right back." Summer headed up the stairs to lay him down.

Autumn looked down as her text alert went off. She rolled her eyes after seeing a number that wasn't programmed. She knew it was only Mason. She blocked his number weeks ago; she was tired of him attempting to contact her. She opened the message and read it.

Unknown number: I've made the decision that, if I can't have you, neither can he. Watch ya back. Ha ha ha ha ha

Autumn's eyes got wide as she screamed, "Oh my god, this nigga is losing it. Look, Hannah." She handed Hannah the phone as Summer and Robert came running down the stairs. Robert had just pulled his T-shirt over his head when they heard Autumn scream. They didn't know what was going on. The way her voice pierced the air; they thought someone may have been outside.

Upon getting downstairs, they saw tears in Autumn's eyes.

"Sis, what's up?" Robert asked as he looked out the front window.

Autumn couldn't answer because she had started crying. Summer sat beside her to console her.

"Here, Robert." Hannah handed the phone to Robert.

He read over the message and became furious. He dialed the number on the screen, and Mason picked up.

"I knew you would call, baby," Mason said.

"Nigga, if you contact my sister again, it will be a problem!" Robert boomed into the phone.

"Who the fuck is this? Is this Ka'ron?" Mason asked, causing Robert to scrunch up his nose.

"Nah, nigga, I said that's my sister. But if you want Ka'ron, I can summon him. I will let you know ahead of time that you barking up the wrong damn tree."

"I'm not scared of that nigga; he snuck me and think he did something."

"Nigga, please. I know for a fact that's a lie. Don't call this fucking phone no more, bitch." Robert hung up the phone before Mason could respond.

He went to kneel in front of Autumn and said, "That nigga talking about Ka'ron? They fought?"

Autumn told Robert and Summer what happened in her dorm. They were surprised because Ka'ron hadn't said anything, but Robert knew that Ka'Ron never put his business out like that.

"Look, Ka'ron needs to know about this message so he can watch his back. I'm going to call him now, baby girl, aight?"

Autumn nodded her head as she wiped her tears. She knew shit was about to get real now.

******

Robert opened the door to his home, and Ka'ron walked in going straight to Autumn. He pulled her from the couch and placed his hands on both sides of her face. He studied her before opening his mouth. He didn't like the terrified look behind her eyes. He wanted her to be worry free, and she couldn't do that with Mason bothering her. He knew the women had a plan, but he was going to step in also.

"I need an address," was all he said after kissing her lips.

"But..."

"No buts, Autumn. I need an address, baby. He hasn't learned his lesson, but he will today."

Autumn knew he wasn't playing. She was just worried about him going to jail or something. She didn't want anything to happen to him, but he wasn't going to take no for an answer.

"He lives in The Park at Oaklawn. When you turn in, it is the second building on the right. He lives downstairs in apartment B in the back."

"Bro, you need me to come with you?" Robert asked with a mouthful of food.

"Nah, I can handle this pee-wee on my own," said Ka'ron before he told Autumn he'd call her later.

"Be careful," Autumn responded just as he placed his hand on the doorknob.

"Always, baby." He walked out the door.

Chapter 32

"Son, have you been okay?" Terry asked Mason.

He and his wife Rhonda had been worried about him. It was the last week of classes before Christmas Break, and he'd been held up in his old room since his parents invited him over. They noticed that he looked rough and not his usual pretty boy self.

"Must be about that girl." Terry noticed his son's body tense up with the mention of Autumn.

He wished that his son realized that everyone wasn't for him. It was obvious that his son messed up and let another man grab her heart. It was time for his son to get that through his head and move on. Terry knew that love was a powerful drug, but he didn't think his son was in love at all judging by the way he treated the girl.

His son wasn't ready to grow up. He still wanted to play the field, and he would rather him do that than to go crazy over a woman who wasn't interested.

"I'm fine, Dad," Mason responded as he rolled his eyes.

"Obviously, you're not. When is the last time you had a haircut, son?"

"I just haven't had time," was his simple reply.

"You need to get up out this room. Your mother is finished with dinner."

"I'll be down in a minute, Dad."

******

Mason pulled up into his apartment complex and backed into the same parking space that he always parked in. He was still thinking about what his father and mother discussed with him. He was tired of people telling him how to feel. He was already beating himself up about the way he had been treating Autumn. He took a good girl for granted. He thought she was one of these weak ass women he was used to messing with, but Autumn proved to be as strong as they came. If he would have taken the time out to meet her family when she used to ask him to, he would have known why.

After Autumn's mother died, she was raised by the strongest woman she knew, her grandmother, and sisters. Being around Robert and Ka'ron also taught her what type of man she should go for. They were perfect examples. Even with Robert making the mistake of sleeping with another woman, he still owned up to his mistake; something that Mason couldn't do. He had too much pride. He was the type of man that thought women should fall to their feet over him.

After sitting in the car for five minutes or so thinking, he finally turned his car off and pulled the keys out the ignition. He opened the door stepping out.

It was nearing ten o'clock at night, and no one was in sight. The chill hit his neck, making the tiny hairs stand up. He assumed it was from the chilly breeze floating through the air. He continued up the sidewalk until he reached his door with his key in hand.

A dark figure emerged from under the stairwell as soon as the key turned to unlock the door. He was heavily in his thoughts and never saw the person coming. Mason was shoved inside, causing him to fall on the stained tan carpet with a gasp. Mason's door was shut and locked as he hurriedly stood to try and defend himself.

The masked figure removed his ski mask and stared at Mason with a wide grin and said, "My people said you were looking for me." Ka'ron slowly made his way over to Mason.

"Get the fuck out!" Mason belted as he frantically searched for something, anything to defend himself with.

"You say that as if I'll actually listen. Don't bitch out now; you was talking all that shit to my brother about me, so what's up?" Ka'ron crossed his masculine arms across his chest with his .45 resting against his chest.

Mason followed Ka'ron's movements before he brought his eyes back to his face. He was pissed inside for being caught off guard. He was even more upset that

Autumn let this nigga know where he lived. If he made it out of this, he was going to teach the little bitch a lesson.

"Put the gun down, and fight me like a man." Mason held his chin up high.

"Oh, now you got some courage?" Ka'ron kept his eyes on Mason as he removed the clip from his gun, dropped it into his wallet, and then put the gun on safety before placing it on Mason's counter.

Mason lunged forward and swung with his right fist, but Ka'ron dodged it and came up with a two piece. Mason touched his lip to find blood on his fingers. That upset him more. He took another swing, and his fist caught Ka'ron's left ear.

"Damn, nigga, you have an issue with putting your hands on a female, but you not doing shit right now," Ka'ron scolded him.

Mason tried his luck again. This time, Ka'ron lifted his leg and did a karate side kick that connected with Mason's knee.

"Ahhh." Mason let out a howl as he fell to the floor. He grabbed his knee right and rolled around on the carpet as Ka'ron grabbed his gun, inserted the clip, and pointed it at Mason's head.

"Now, this is how this shit will go. Do not call Autumn; do not talk to her. If you see her, turn the other way. If you tell someone I did this to you, I will kill you. Do you understand?"

Mason didn't answer because of the pain rushing through his leg. Because Mason wasn't answering quick enough, Ka'ron lifted his foot and came down on his right leg as hard as he could. The sound his knee made when it cracked caused Ka'ron's stomach to churn and Mason to scream at the top of his lungs.

"Ye- Yes. I hear you, man; please, I need to get some help," Mason screeched.

Satisfied, Ka'ron lowered his gun before saying, "Good, now I'm going to fuck my woman and put her to sleep." He chuckled at the look of death Mason was giving him before disappearing out the door.

Chapter 33

A sea of blue and gold could be seen by everyone who filled the stadium. The running back had just made a touchdown, which caused the band to play loudly letting number twenty-three know it was a job well done. The time clock just hit zero in the second quarter, meaning the first half was over, and it was time for the greatest halftime show on earth.

"Y'all ready to put on this show?" Dr. Willie screamed out as the band made their way from the bleachers to the sideline of the field.

"Who are we?" Dr. Willie shouted.

"The Marching Golden Bulls. The baddest band in the land," the band screamed in unison right before the drums started the cadence for the band to march out onto the field and give the best show they knew how.

Once everyone was in formation, the drum major took the field and did his dance before the band played their first note. The crowd was going wild hyping the band up to do their thing. The melody to "Disco Inferno" by The Trammps could be heard as the band marched and formed J.C.S.U on the field. The crowd continued to scream as the flag girls and dancers formed a '17 at the bottom of the band's formation. It was lit in the stadium. The onlookers were dancing and singing the lyrics to the song and were having a good time.

The music stopped as the drums played their solo before breaking out into the next song "Formation" by Beyoncé. Autumn smiled with her back straight twirling her flag as she marched to her next spot on the field. She searched the bleachers and laid eyes on her family where they always sat.

Everyone was there, even her nieces and nephews. They all had their hands in the air, even the babies with the help of their parents, it was so cute. Autumn's family were her biggest supporters.

"J.C.S.Uuuuuu," the band chanted before ending their show.

"Who are we?" the band screamed out.

The crowd responded as they always did, yelling out, "J.C.S.Uuuu."

The band marched all the way back to their section in the bleachers. The game went on, and The Golden Bulls won against Livingstone College forty to thirty-one. The crowd went wild as the football team celebrated.

The melody to "We are the Champions" could be heard as the band played the song while marching across campus back to the band facility. Once they were in front of the building, the drum major gave the "at ease" command and dismissed the band.

Everyone cheered as they hugged each other for a job well done. There would be no more games; however,, the band had two competitions before band season was completely over.

******

"I'm so proud of you, Autumn. You are doing a great job juggling school, the band, and your personal life, I'm just proud of you. We all are," Wynter expressed how proud she was of her little sister as they sat at the table at Maggie's house, enjoying the feast that she prepared.

Autumn sat with tears in her eyes. It meant a lot to her that her family thought highly of her.

"Thank you," she whispered.

Ka'ron wiped her tears away and said, "I'm proud of you too, baby girl." He smiled at her.

"Okay, okay, stop with the mushy stuff," Autumn said, causing laughter to fill the room.

Dinner was great. Bellies were full and the whole family had the 'itis. You know when you are so full off that good food that all you want to do is sleep.

"Hey, let's play Catch Phrase," Roman, Wynter's husband shouted.

"Ooo yes, we haven't played that in a while." Summer stood to retrieve the game from the hallway closet.

The family used to play games all the time, but with everyone having their separate lives, they hadn't played in awhile.

Everyone formed a circle in the living room, bringing in a few chairs from the kitchen to connect between the loveseat and couch. Every other person was on the same team. The timer started, and the game began. Robert was up first.

"Okay, it flies in the sky," Robert yelled out.

"A plane," Maggie answered.

"No, it can carry a message and could be pulled by a plane."

"A blimp," Wynter screamed.

"Yes." Robert passed the game to Summer.

"Okay, when you are running in slow motion," she yelled, looking directly at her sister.

"A jog," Autumn answered.

"Yes." She hurriedly passed the game to Roman.

"One of the biggest states. Cowboys."

"Texas," everyone on his team screamed.

They kept passing the game until the buzzer went off. It was a great evening for the Harts and friends. This is what it was all about: family. Autumn loved her family and wouldn't let anyone else in her life that wasn't worthy to be around her family.

Wynter and her family were the first to leave. Her and Roman bundled their children up to protect them from the night air, gave everyone a hug, and then they were out the door. Summer and Robert did the same. Lastly, Autumn and Ka'ron were the last to leave once she decided to go home with him. Maggie was smiling from ear to ear watching the two lovebirds.

"What you smiling for, Memaw?" Autumn asked.

"Y'all are just so cute. It's about time you two went for what you want and deserve," Memaw responded.

Autumn giggled as Ka'ron kissed her on the cheek and agreed with her grandma.

Chapter 34

The room was dark and smelled of old corn chips and stinking ass. It had been this way through Christmas and now the New Year since Mason's knee was fractured by Ka'ron. He was in the dumps; he barely wanted to eat. He was going to miss the rest of indoor track season, maybe even outdoor season, and he wasn't happy about that.

His father was upset because he didn't believe Mason's story about him falling directly on his knee on the concrete while playing basketball. He had a feeling that someone did this to his son. Little did he know, he was correct, but out of fear of what Ka'ron may do, Mason would never tell his father the truth.

Mason groaned as he heard his room door in his parents' house creep open. He had to move back in with them because he couldn't stay alone at the moment. Luckily, his lease was up on his apartment, and there was no need to renew it. His father and a couple of his friends packed everything and put everything he wouldn't need in storage. Mason prayed his father wouldn't find his steroids. Terry hadn't bought it up, making him realize that his father indeed didn't see them. If he did, he would have been up in his face already.

"Mason, you need to eat, baby. I cooked you up something," Rhonda, his mother's, soft voice penetrated his ears.

His mother was the sweetest woman he knew. For that reason, he wouldn't disrespect her by telling her to get the hell out his room. That's what he wanted to say though. Mason didn't feel like being bothered at all. He just wanted to lay in his room and cut off the outside world. Instead, he slowly slid to the head of the bed, careful not to move his leg too much.

"Thanks, Ma," he solemnly replied as she placed the tray of cheese grits, an omelet, and sausage across his lap.

His stomach grumbled as a reminder that he hadn't eaten since some time yesterday. This would be his first time eating a real meal.

Rhonda sat on the edge of the bed after removing a can of sprite from her robe pocket and placing on the nightstand.

"Are you still not going to tell us the truth, Mason? Whoever did this needs to pay," Rhonda expressed sadly.

Mason placed a spoonful of his grits before saying, "That is the truth, Ma. I hate I was being so careless, but it happened. I knew I couldn't dunk that damn ball."

Rhonda studied his eyes as Mason looked back at her. All she saw was deception but decided to leave it alone. She knew he wouldn't tell them until he was ready; if he was ever ready. Rhonda nodded her head and then stood to leave the room. She was disappointed in her son; he was protecting someone, and Rhonda had her qualms of who it was.

Mason finished most of his breakfast and sat the tray on the other side of his bed. He carefully swung his legs over the side of the bed and reached for his crutches to assist him. Normally, he would transfer from his bed to the wheelchair, but the bathroom was two feet away. He carefully stood, only placing pressure on his right leg to stand. He hopped to the bathroom and used the crutches to help hold himself up as he used the bathroom. After washing his hands, he went back to bed to sulk in his own problems.

Mason was angry inside. He was angry at Autumn for leaving him and causing the train of events in his life. He was mad at Ka'ron for stepping to his girl and taking her away. He was mad at his father for being too hard on him and leading him to drugs. Lastly, he was mad at himself for allowing a bitch to take over his mind the way that Autumn did. The more that Mason laid around, the more he realized that he couldn't let Autumn and Ka'ron get away with what they'd done to him. His father got a pass because that's his father, but not the other two. His body molded into the mattress as he closed his eyes and dreamed about what he would do to them. A smile crossed his face as different thoughts crossed his mind.

******

School had been back in session for a month. It was the first week of February, and the band had just finished practicing their show for the Honda Classic Band Competition that would be held in Atlanta.

Autumn tapped Jalisa on her shoulder when she walked past her. Jalisa stopped to see what she wanted.

"Hey, you heard what happened to Mason?" Autumn asked.

"Yeah, that's what his ass gets. He is back. I've seen him in a wheelchair at first, but now he is on crutches. They are saying his track career may be over if he can't run for outdoor season."

Autumn had no idea; she purposely stayed away from all conversations concerning Mason since she was the reason he couldn't use his legs at the moment. Ka'ron told her everything. The sad part was, she had no sympathy for him.

"Damn, it is unfortunate. But, hey, he must have pissed someone off. Are you still looking to press charges?" Autumn inquired.

"Well, truthfully, some of us thought that him not being able to run is worse than what may happen to him if he were arrested. Track and field is his life. Without that, he is nothing. However, I do have a lawyer who is in the process of speaking to some of the ladies just in case. It's three right now. Four if you give a statement."

"Okay, I feel you. If it comes down to it, I'm in," Autumn agreed.

"Thank you so much, Autumn. I know we got off to a rocky start, but I never really disliked you. If anything, people are jealous of you. You have it all. You are on the dean's list, you on the squad, you are beautiful, and now you have a man who loves you. Everyone can tell every time he comes here. I'm sorry for giving you trouble."

"Thanks for that, Jalisa. It means a lot." Autumn smiled and gave Jalisa a high-five before they went their separate ways.

Chapter 35

Autumn and Hannah finished working on their paper in the library and then packed their belongings and prepared to leave. Autumn pulled her coat on, followed by gloves and her thick headband to cover her ears from the cold that she knew was waiting for her outside. Hannah did the same. After securing their book bag on their shoulders, they headed for the door.

Autumn's eyebrows dipped, and her lip curled in confusion as they stepped out to see three members of the dance team dancing to about twenty members of the band playing "Crazy in Love" by Beyoncé.

Autumn tried to walk around them but was stopped by a smiling Hannah. Autumn looked up to see more members of the dance team join in. By the time the whole dance team, including the auxiliary squad, joined, Autumn realized it was a flash mob.

"What is this?" she turned to Hannah and asked confusingly.

"Just watch," was Hannah's simple reply.

Autumn noticed more and more people joining. It was at least one hundred people covering the dead grass.

Autumn glanced to the left of her as her family hurriedly joined in for the last sixteen counts. At this point, she had tears in her eyes. When the flash mob was over, there was a big sign asking, *Will you go steady with me?* And the snare drums continued to roll.

The crowd moved to both sides and made way for Ka'ron. He coolly walked down the cleared space in a pair of faded black jeans with a pair of black Timberlands and a black button up shirt with a gray peacoat. In his hand, he held red roses. He looked real debonair. Upon standing in front of Autumn, he handed her the roses as tears cascaded down her face.

No man had ever gone the extra mile for her. She gazed into his eyes lovingly, not wanting this moment to pass. He stared back with his pearly whites showing before pulling out a small ring box. He grabbed her hand and said, "You already know what you mean to me. On this Valentine's Day, I want to make you a promise that, once you graduate, you will get an even bigger and better ring to become my fiancée. Until then, I'm rockin' with only you, baby girl. So what's up, you down?"

"Hell yeah I am!" Autumn waited until he placed the ring on her finger before jumping into his arms. They pecked each other's lips a few times before Autumn turned to Hannah and punched her in the arm.

"You knew. Oh my god, I can't believe you kept this from me."

Hannah giggled and responded, "It was a surprise, duh."

Autumn then turned to her sisters and her grandmother and gave them a hug. Autumn couldn't believe that her friend helped orchestrate all of this for her. This was the best day ever.

"Okay, baby, we have plans. I have it all laid out. No need to go back to your room. I have everything that you will need."

******

Autumn emerged from the shower and was still in a good mood from the events of earlier. When they got to Ka'ron's house, there were shopping bags sitting near the door. She was so excited after peeking inside that she hurriedly got undressed to shower. She was eager to get to where they were going. She heard that Firebirds was a great restaurant and was ready to see for herself.

She glanced up at Ka'ron who was only in a towel. He took a shower in the hallway bathroom because he knew that, if he would have joined her, they would be late for their reservations. Autumn licked her lips at the man standing before her. She had to shake her head from the impure thoughts circulating in her head. This man was a masterpiece, and his sexy ass was all hers. They both dressed in silence and were ready to get the night over with so that they could each show the other how they really felt by making love to each other's body.

Autumn pulled a pair of distressed, denim jeans over her curvy hips. They had holes in them, which were filled with black cloth. They fit her perfectly; she wondered how he knew her exact size. She then pulled a thin black and gray sweater over her head before sticking her legs into the black stiletto knee boots that he purchased to wear over her jeans. She glanced at the closet door which had a black pea coat hanging on it which wasn't there before. He did good picking out her few outfits. She glanced over at him smiling. She felt butterflies inside when looking at him that she hoped never went away.

"I have something else for you," he told her as he pulled his own jeans over his ass before stepping into his gray, suede Timberland boots.

"There's more? What is it?" she asked, looking around to see if she could spot another gift.

"Finish getting dressed, and you shall see," he responded as he lifted his button-up shirt draping his shoulders with it and covering his t-shirt.

Autumn kissed Ka'ron before turning on her heels and heading to the bathroom. It took her thirty minutes to apply a light coat of makeup and to do her hair. She parted her hair on the side and let it hang to one side, using a bobbie pin to be sure the opposite side of her hair didn't fall in her face and wouldn't fall down. She picked up a pair of earrings to put on when she heard Ka'ron instruct her to wait a minute. He handed her another jewelry box, which held a pair of diamond stud earrings.

"I love these; thank you," she thanked him as he grabbed the earring and placed them in her ear.

He then handed her another box, which held a necklace with a diamond K on it.

"Who told you I wanted to wear a necklace with a 'K' on it?" Her face was scrunched up as she tried not to laugh.

"Girl, stop and turn around so I can put this necklace on your ass." He laughed, causing her to laugh as well.

She went into her purse and pulled out a gift for him. Although he wasn't expecting anything, he was grateful for his gift. He opened the box and pulled out a black Fossil digital smart watch. He smiled from ear to ear.

"This is dope, babe." He admired the watch before taking off the one he currently had on and replaced it with the new one. He walked up to her and placed his arms on her lower back. He kissed her a few times as a thank you before handing her, her coat and before putting on his own, then they were out the door.

******

The restaurant atmosphere was laid back. The ambiance was beautiful, and Autumn was pleased. The couple sat across from each other, sipping wine and eating jumbo shrimp as they waited on their main dish.

"What's on your mind, baby?" Ka'ron asked.

"I just can't believe you did all of this for me. Well, I can but still." She laughed before continuing. "Whose idea was the flash mob?

"Hannah suggested it, but I thought it was a good idea. She suggested we have the music playing over the loudspeakers outside, but I thought it would be more personal using the band and dance team since you love the band so much. It wasn't hard getting everyone to participate. However, some of the girls took some convincing. Katrina was salty and was the only one who wasn't there."

"Oh well." Autumn shrugged, not caring one way or another if someone didn't participate. Nothing or no one would ruin her day.

The waitress came and sat Ka'ron's prime steak and Autumn's wood grilled salmon down. They both had lobster tail and asparagus on their plates.

"This looks sooo good." Autumn admired her plate.

"Damn sure do." Ka'ron cut off a piece of the tender and juicy looking steak, pulling it off the fork with his teeth. "Mmm. Damn, you want to taste a piece, baby?"

Autumn nodded her head, and he cut another small piece and held his fork up to her mouth so that she could pull it off with her teeth.

"Oh wow." She cut a piece of salmon and did the same and let him taste it.

Dinner was cool; they ate and talked about everything under the sun. She loved how he was so interested in her education. She asked him questions about his job and future plans in return. Once dinner was over, they were glad to be back home.

They weren't in the house good before Ka'ron backed Autumn against the front door pressing his lips against hers as he gripped her shirt and pulled it over her head; they released the hold on each other's lips for only a second. She then gripped each side of his shirt and ripped it open, causing the buttons to pop before he let it fall down his arms before she lifted his t-shirt over his head.

"Damn, girl. You strong arming a nigga," he said as he reached behind her to unsnap her bra before attacking her nipple, causing her head to fall back in pleasure. They struggled to unbutton each other's jeans. Autumn was trying so hard that she fell over to the side and tried to step out of them.

"Oh my god." She covered her face while Ka'ron snickered as he bent over to remove her pants and panties. After removing his own, he picked her up and carried her to his bedroom. He gently laid her on the bed and gazed into her eyes.

"I love yo' sexy ass, man." He kissed her neck and made a trail all the way to her treasure as she confessed her love for him.

"Oooooo," she cried out as he inserted his tongue in her most sacred place. Entering his long finger into her and giving her the most euphoric feeling, he pulled an orgasm right out of her. Ka'ron's dick felt as if it was going to crack if he didn't slide up in her warm hole. He slid his sweaty body back up as he stroked himself to relieve some of the pressure built up. After placing one leg over his shoulder and pressing the other as wide as her leg could go against the mattress, he slowly entered her and commenced to making love to his woman all night. This was about to be one beautiful weekend.

Chapter 36

Autumn lifted herself from the mattress, stretched her arms over her head as she yawned, and then swung her legs over the side of the bed before standing. She was in a great mood from the weekend that she shared with her man. She was in awe the whole weekend and did not want the weekend to end.

She stepped toward the bathroom, but out of the corner of her eyes, she saw an envelope that looked as if it were slid under the door. She grabbed it and then went into the bathroom, pulling down her shorts along with her panties before plopping down on the toilet. Noticing that the envelope was addressed to her, she tore it open to see what the review board wanted with her.

"What the fuck?" she shrieked, not believing what she was reading.

"How could this be?" She placed the letter on the sink so that she could wipe herself and then pulled up her panties and shorts.

Picking the letter back up, she went to sit on her bed to study the letter better. She couldn't believe what she was looking at. She was being asked to come to student affairs to sit in front of the dean of students along with other faculty members today. She was being accused of plagiarism. She knew there was no way she copied anyone's work. She worked tirelessly on her essay on *The Effects of Childhood Education and Becoming an Adult*. She was excited about the paper. She wanted to be a teacher for goodness sakes; why would she play with her own education like that?

A tear slipped down the side of her face as she picked up the phone to call Ka'ron. He was the first person she thought about telling since Hannah was already in her first class for the day.

"What's up, baby girl?"

"Ka'ron…" She spoke softly, causing him to perk up at the strain in her voice.

"What's up? You okay?" he asked.

"Somebody is trying to ruin me," she stated as she read the letter to him.

Without giving it a thought, he told her that he was on his way and for her to get ready. It didn't take long for Autumn to get dressed. As soon as she put her shoes on, Ka'ron was at the door engulfing her in his arms. He knew how much school meant to her and hoped that this was just a misunderstanding. He knew she would never plagiarize anything.

"What am I going to do?" she cried on his shoulder.

"Listen, baby, we don't know anything yet. We have thirty minutes to get across campus. Dry your face so we can go see what's going on. I got you." He smiled as he kissed her tears away.

Autumn's palms were sweaty, and her right leg shook as her and Ka'ron sat outside the student affairs' office and waited on her name to be called. Ka'ron held her hand tightly and tried to reassure her that everything would be okay. Even if not at this moment, the truth always came out.

"Autumn Hart."

Her name was finally called. She stood and turned to Ka'ron who stood with her. He kissed her on the forehead and gave her a stern look to hold it together. She turned around with a smile and followed the dean into the room. She sat in the chair designated for her and waited for the meeting to begin.

"Hello, Ms. Hart," Dean Witherspoon greeted.

"Hello, Dean Witherspoon, Professor, ma'am," Autumn greeted everyone.

"We will get straight to it since I assume you read the letter you received in its entirety?" the dean raised her eyebrow, and when Autumn nodded her head, she continued.

"We received notification that you did not write this paper and instead copied right off the internet. We did our research and saw that this paper indeed was that of a previous student who was entered into a writing contest."

A copy of Autumn's alleged paper and the supposed paper she copied from was slid across the table to her. Autumn was already shaking her head and was disagreeing with what was being said. She could already tell by the cover sheet that this paper was not hers. It has the wrong date on it. She then turned to the next page but closed it after reading the first line.

"This isn't mine. I don't know how you guys received this, but it's not mine. The correct date isn't even on the front. Professor, you know me. You know this isn't something I would do," Autumn plead.

"Yes, Ms. Hart, and I am surprised at this whole thing. I thought this was a mistake. Do you have your copy, or can you pull it up on this laptop on your cloud?"

Autumn nodded her head as she grabbed the laptop and signed in to her Microsoft OneDrive. She sat up straight with wide eyes after pressing button after button.

"What?!" she shrieked.

"This can't be." She looked up toward the Dean with tears in her eyes and said, "My entire cloud has been deleted." She turned the laptop around before she said, "Everything I have been working on is gone. Wiped clean."

Dean Witherspoon looked at the laptop screen with a straight face. She, along with everyone sitting in front of

Autumn, was shocked at the revelation that Autumn may have cheated. Although they believed her, without proof, as per school rules, nothing could be done.

"Ms. Hart, while I understand that this may not be your doing, until you find that paper, we have to suspend you from the university. But, to be fair, we will give you until the end of the day to find a printed copy, restore your OneDrive, or maybe you also saved it to a thumb drive. If not, as of tomorrow, you are suspended until further notice."

Autumn stopped listening at the word suspended. She started off as different scenarios of what could have happened. She then started thinking of where her thumb drive could be. She was sure she saved it there, but where did she put it? She didn't want to be a bitch and get an attitude with the adults in front of her, so she simply thanked them with tears in her eyes and hoped that she could find that thumb drive.

She walked out of the room into Ka'ron's waiting arms. She explained what she needed to do for her to not be suspended. He agreed to help her look for her thumb drive. He grabbed her hand and led her out the door.

Mason stood on the side of the building with a smile on his face. He saw the angry expression on Ka'ron's face and the sad expression on Autumn's as soon as they hit the door. He stepped back until they passed him, and then he watched as Ka'ron consoled her as they walked.

Mason turned and used his crutch to walk the other way. He thought about all he did to prepare for this day. It was genius, and he was glad that he had a computer whiz as a friend to help him out.

"I'd like to see her get out of this shit," he gloated

******

Three days later, Autumn laid in Ka'ron's bed and waited for him to return from work. She was depressed and hadn't spoken to anyone. The only person that knew she was suspended was Ka'ron and Hannah. She continued to look for her thumb drive, but sometimes, she got so sad that she only wanted to lay around. She just didn't understand who would do this to her.

Autumn sat up in the bed with a loud gasp as Mason came to mind. She didn't think of it before because she was so upset. She remembered Mason having a friend who could hack into anything. She would bet her last dollar that Mason did this to her. He knew her schedule and knew about the assignment because it was given out while her and Mason were still together.

She jumped up when she heard Ka'ron coming through the front door.

"Baby, I know what happened, and who did it," she explained before searching every inch of Ka'ron's bedroom, including the bags he bought her for Valentine's. Then she remembered her coat. She ran to the closet and looked in the inside pocket.

"Bingo."

Chapter 37

The Mercedes-Benz Stadium in Atlanta Georgia was filled to capacity. The roar of the crowd was an indication that the Johnson C. Smith Golden Bull's Band did an amazing job with their performance. Autumn couldn't help but smile at the fact that she was still awarded the opportunity to participate.

The day that she found her thumb drive, her and Ka'ron rushed over to the University and went straight to the dean's office. They made it right in time because Dean Witherspoon was packing up to leave for the day. Autumn was so excited that she didn't bother putting on any real clothes. Ka'ron joked the whole ride and let her know she looked like a bag of Skittles. She had on a pair of red and pink sweatpants from Victoria's Secret, a yellow tank top, his royal blue Ralph Lauren Coat, which was too big, and let's not forget about her beige UGG Boots. She was still cute but looked a mess, but she did not give a care in the world.

They sat in the waiting area for thirty minutes before her professor was able to make it down. Her professor sat and read half of her paper and was thoroughly impressed.

Autumn was promised that she would have her grade by the end of the day.

Dean Witherspoon immediately reinstated Autumn and congratulated her on a job well done based off her professor's words. Autumn was ecstatic and promised to make up all the work she missed from every class. She had about a week's worth of work to complete, but she had no issues doing so. Autumn loved school and always strived to be the best.

That day, Autumn informed the dean of everything concerning Mason with Ka'ron's encouragement. The dean was flabbergasted at the allegations. She promised to look into the matter and deal out whatever consequences that went along with the crime. Autumn gave Jalisa's name and informed Dean Witherspoon that, if she searched, there would be other women.

After only a week, all information was gathered on Mason. He was arrested on campus leaving one of his classes. He wasn't on crutches any more but had a brace on his knee. Five women came forward when the dean put word out. He was facing two to three years in prison and would have to register as a sex offender if he was found guilty. He, of course, was expelled, and his track career was over. No Olympic trials for him. His mother and father were so disappointed in him, but of course, they would be there for their son. After discussing with them how he felt all these years and the lengths he went through to please his parents, they realized that they were always too hard on him and should have been proud of him no matter what.

At this point, Autumn didn't care what happened to Mason. He tried to ruin her life by attempting to get her expelled from school. As Maggie once told her, God had her back, and no one could take away what was meant for her.

"J.C.S.Uuuuuuuuu," the band chanted as they filed back into the stands.

The competition went on for another four hours before the winners were announced.

"And lastly, first place overall performance goes to…"

Every drum in the stadium played a roll for fifteen seconds before the announcer said, "From Charlotte, North Carolina, Johnson C. Smith Universityyyyyyy."

The band screamed joyfully. They did good bringing in first place in auxiliary, drumline, and overall. Second place was awarded for the dance team. Once they finished enjoying themselves, they headed to the bus so they could head back to the hotel since they would be spending the night and heading home the next day.

It was so many people that Autumn didn't get to see her family until they were back at the hotel. She let the band director know that she was going to be with her family and would be riding back with them also. The first person she saw was Ka'ron. She ran up to him and jumped into his arms, causing him to wrap her in his arms and tightly kiss her on the cheek.

"Dang, that's the only person you see? A girl get a man in her life and forgets all about her family," her sister, Wynter, said, causing everyone to laugh.

Autumn then hugged everyone before going up to her room to change. The family planned to go to Pappadeaux in an hour.

******

"You did great out there," Ka'ron said as he grabbed Autumn's hand and walked into the restaurant.

"I was like, that's my girl." Ka'ron cupped his mouth acting as if he were shouting, causing Autumn to laugh and bump him with her hip.

"What did I do? Give me a kiss." He bent down so that their lips could connect before he grabbed the door and opened it.

The family was already seated. Autumn and Ka'ron were late because he swore he just had to feel her insides once she walked out the bathroom butt ass naked. Of course, she wasn't going to object.

"We're here," Autumn announced smiling as they were led to their waiting family by the hostess.

"It's about damn time with y'all nasty asses." Maggie rolled her eyes jokingly.

"What?" Autumn had a sly expression on her face. "I had to shower and everything," she expressed as Ka'ron laid her coat and his own on the backs of their chairs before taking his seat.

Everyone knew they were full of shit but decided not to say anything else as the two made googly eyes at each other. Once the waitress walked around the table and took everyone's order, Autumn and her family discussed everything under the sun, including Mason and her getting suspended. Maggie and her sisters were upset but were proud she was able to handle it.

Autumn glanced around the table at the people she knew for a fact loved her. The people she knew would be there for her no matter what. Her eyes then landed on Ka'ron, who was staring right back and was admiring her in his own thoughts. He grabbed her hand and kissed the back of it, causing her brown skin to turn a shade of red. Yes, they had seven years between them, but their love for each other was on the same level.

Autumn had been through hell with Mason. What she thought was love never was. Autumn had to go through lust in order to find true love. Mason's season led her right to the man she was truly meant to be with.

"I love you," Autumn whispered.

"I love you too, baby girl."

Autumn wouldn't change this experience for the world. She learned a valuable lesson about life; some people are only meant to be in it for a season.

The End... For Now

Note from Author

I hope you all enjoyed this love story. I know I enjoyed writing it. I love all of my readers and it's because of you guys that I continue to write these stories.

Seasons of Love is a three book series based on three sisters; Summer, Autumn, and Wynter.
Each book will be focused on one sister with the others having supporting scenes.
Each sister goes through trials and tribulations that they must overcome for true love. They must realize that everyone isn't meant to be in your life forever and also that people make mistakes and can change.
All three books are now available...

I love keeping in touch with my readers. You guys are awesome!

Facebook: Quisha Dynae's Readers
Instagram: Quisha_dynae
Twitter: @quishadynae
E-mail: Quishadynae@yahoo.com

Other books by Quisha Dynae

-Bad Boys Ain't no Good: Good Boys Ain't no Fun

-Not Gon' Cry

-Love the Way You Lie

-Side Nigga

-Loving Him Through it all: Yancey and Ariel

-Selfish With Your Love

-Loving me Unconditionally: A Boss B*tch Love Story

-Sydney Valentine

-Loving You Hurts Me

-Captivated by a Queen City Killa

-She Fell for a F*ck Boy

-Entangled in his Hood Love 1-2

-Loving a Thug on Valentine's Day

-His Essence Her Peace

-A Hustla's Promise

-A Hustla's Vow

-Seasons of Love: Summer's Story

-Seasons of Love: Wynter's Story

All books available on Amazon.com